3

$\rho$

)12

# Two For Texas

The Texas cattle town of Buckeye has been taken over by outlaw boss Wade Garvey. When his men start turning up with their throats cut, he brings in the hired gunfighter known as Nevado to find the killer.

But all is not what it seems in Buckeye where simmering passions lead to the unlikely liaison between Nevado and the mysterious knife-wielder. It all culminates in an explosive climax on Nob Hill: a breath-taking finale to an exciting tale of the Old West.

# Two for Texas

Ethan Flagg

**A Black Horse Western**

ROBERT HALE · LONDON

© Ethan Flagg 2008
First published in Great Britain 2008

ISBN 978-0-7090-8611-6

Robert Hale Limited
Clerkenwell House
Clerkenwell Green
London EC1R 0HT

www.halebooks.com

The right of Ethan Flagg to be identified as
author of this work has been asserted by him
in accordance with the Copyright, Designs and
Patents Act 1988

Typeset by
Derek Doyle & Associates, Shaw Heath
Printed and bound in Great Britain by
CPI Antony Rowe, Chippenham, Wiltshire

# ONE

# BUFFALOED

'Urrrrgh!'

A racking groan issued from tightly pursed lips as the big man struggled to raise himself. Gingerly he patted the source of his anguish where an ugly lump had sprouted on the crown of his head. Some unknown assailant must have laid him out. The long hair, white as snow, was now contaminated a dark red where dried blood had caked over the wound.

He winced at the touch.

Slowly he peered around, nose puckering in disgust. What kind of smelly dump was this? The acrid reek came from a bucket in the corner. And it had obviously not been emptied since the previous occupant's residence in this elegant abode.

Beams of light filtered between a trio of thick steel

window bars outlining the bare walls. Scratched into the peeling adobe were the marks made by an erstwhile incumbent. Roughly sketched gallows at the end indicated how long the poor sap had to go before his meeting with the official neck-stretcher.

So that was it: he was in jail!

A high-pitched twitter drew his gritty peepers back to the window where a meadowlark was cockily appraising him. The two eyed one another. Seeing no likelihood of breakfast from this sorry specimen, the bird emitted a scornful cheep. A final ruffle of its plumage, and it was airborne leaving the prisoner even more aware of his unfortunate predicament.

Then another sound cut through his distorted ruminations, grating further on the prisoner's already sensitive nerves. The man screwed up his leathery features attempting to block out the vibrating cacophony that threatened to blow his head off. Rheumy eyes lifted whilst attempting to focus on a tin cup rattling the bars of the cell door.

'Finally woke up, have yuh?'

Another throaty gurgle was the sole response to the sharp query.

'Better drink this,' added the same gruff voice whilst laying the half-empty mug on the cell floor. 'It'll help sober you up. You got visitors.'

Picking up the mug of coffee, now half empty, the prisoner tossed the contents down his gullet. He had tasted better, but at least the bitter concoction served to loosen up his brain cells.

'What in the name of a Texas tornado am I doing

in this dump?' he enquired of the grizzled law dog. Shaking his head, he tried to dispel the clutching torpor that threatened to plunge him back into oblivion; the result of hard liquor and an even harder gun butt. Another slurp of the muddy dregs swilling around the tin mug and he was finally able to stand upright.

A set of uneven snappers, yellowed by too much baccy chewing, grinned back at him. The owner hawked a lump of brown goo towards the cell's slop bucket. Even without looking, his aim was uncannily accurate.

Jubal Cade had once been a renowned and well-respected town-tamer. People stepped out of his way when he walked down the street. After the war when the cattle trade was in its infancy, Cade had proved his worth in numerous end-of-trail camps. A heavy fist and a slick gun arm were more than enough to discourage the troublesome riff raff that were attracted to such bergs like flies to a dung heap.

But that was a long time ago. Good living had taken its toll and a slack belly and rotund girth were the inevitable result. Now he was only too glad of a job rolling drunks in this remote backwater of west Texas.

'Can't yuh remember then?' he smirked, working his jaws against the cud.

'Think I'd be asking if I could?' came back the terse response.

'You was over in the War Bonnet saloon.' The

lawman paused eyeing his prisoner, enjoying the memory game. 'These two buffalo skinners were giving you some grief. Remember now?'

The prisoner screwed up his tired eyes striving to recall the incident. Slowly through the hazy mist of pain that still gripped his throbbing head, the grim details from the previous night began to filter through the grey matter.

A pall of smoke hung in the fetid air of the drinking parlour, the result of a cloying mix of fatty oil lamps, tobacco and alcohol fumes. At the bar, a tall stranger stood hunched over a glass of warm beer. It was his second. To his right hand was a small half-empty glass of bourbon.

The man had been on the trail since first light and reckoned he had earned the right to slake his thirst.

'Come far, stranger? You look to me like you could use a good meal. The War Bonnet serves the best chilli in town. Comfortable rooms as well if it's accommodation you're after.'

'Just do your job and and stow the advertisin'.'

The tight-lipped response to the bartender's questioning made it clear to all within earshot that the guy didn't welcome company and wanted to be left alone.

Clad in dust-caked trail gear, the one thing that set him apart from other drinkers was the snow-white hair hanging shoulder-length beneath the low-crowned plainsman hat. Others had noticed the distinctive feature and recognized that here was a guy not to be messed with. Or maybe it was the tooled leather gunbelt tied low on his right hip with the ivory butt of a .44 Colt Frontier poking out that told its own tale.

In consequence, he was given a wide berth.

All that is except by two scruffy buffalo skinners who figured the evening needed livening up.

Buck Jenkins was heavy-set and sported a straggly black beard badly in need of a trim. His partner, Chet Farlow, was clad in greasy buckskins. Thin and waspish, he had the unmistakable look of a hungry gopher. Unceremoniously, Jenkins dug an elbow into his partner's ribs. With a sly wink, he edged along the bar, at the same time loosening the .36 Navy Colt strapped to his right thigh.

'Where you hidin' the dwarves then, mister?'

The taut question, issued with a malicious chortle, cut through the heady atmosphere. It was obvious to all that it was aimed at the tall stranger. A silence descended over the interior of the saloon. Ignoring the acerbic jibe, he slowly lifted the beer glass to his lips.

To everybody in the room, it appeared as if he hadn't heard. Although a close observer might have witnessed a steely glint flicker in the man's grey eyes, plus a tightening of the firm jawline.

'You deaf, or just plain stupid?' scowled Jenkins who had expected some reaction to his vexatious provocation. He stood square on to the bar no more than three feet from the man.

Without turning his head, the man replied in barely more than a whisper, 'You talking to me, dipshit?'

Jenkins bristled at the insult, then laughed mirthlessly. 'You're Snow White, ain't yuh? So where are the dwarves?'

Farlow was the only other person in the saloon who seemed to find this remark amusing. He chuckled uproariously.

'There's supposed to be seven, ain't there?' he scoffed.

'The name's Nevado,' hissed the stranger.

'What sort of dago name is that?' snarled Jenkins, jabbing a finger at his adversary. 'Nobody with hair that colour should be called anything other than Snow White.'

'Here we go again,' muttered Nevado under his breath.

A sigh of irritation hissed from between clenched teeth. Why couldn't these skunks just leave him alone? Ever since he had been knee-high to a grasshopper, he had been tormented about his white hair. Schooldays back in Kentucky were remembered as a succession of fights to avoid being labelled a milksop. Everybody knew the story of Snow White.

What was even worse was the fact that his real name was Stanley Black. What had he done to deserve such an irksome burden?

He had tried shaving it all off, but it kept growing back. In the end, one persecutor had stepped over the mark and had paid the ultimate price.

That was his first killing. It would not be the last. Ultimately, Stanley decided to embrace his unwanted hair colour calling himself Nevado which was Spanish for snow-bound.

He kept his true reason for coming west under a tight wrap, but figured that folks on the Texas frontier would be more tolerant of a man's imperfections. More inclined to accept a person for what he was and how he behaved. But it seemed that he had thought wrong. There would always be those who sought to humiliate others whom they considered easy game.

And guys like these never knew when to cut their losses and retire.

Nevado slowly turned his head. Languidly, he deigned to acknowledge the presence of the burly ruffian.

'Now if you've had your fun, I suggest you back off.' He sniffed the air meaningfully. 'And get a bath while you're at it. You smell worse than a pig's midden.'

A manic growl issued from the gawping maw of the blustering tough.

'No pesky white owl speaks to me like that.'

He lunged towards his adversary intending to lay him out with a slicing haymaker. Had it connected, that would have been the end of the contest.

Nevado swayed back on his heels allowing the flailing swing to zip past. His left hand still gripped the beer glass, the contents of which were immediately upended into Jenkins's face.

The dripping bruiser staggered back in shock. For the moment he was out of the picture.

Now it was Farlow's turn. Sliding under his partner's trailing arm, he came in low. His left hand slid behind his back where a lethal bowie knife was concealed. But he wasn't fast enough. A jolting uppercut crashed into his stubbly chin. Teeth rattled like an angry sidewinder as the little weasel was lifted two feet off the floor.

Howling like an itchy coyote, he tottered backwards, sprawling across a table and scattering the abandoned card game in all directions.

Buck Jenkins was no slouch when it came to the rough stuff. He quickly shook off the effects of the dousing.

'Time to say yer prayers, Snowy,' he snarled, making a grab for his holstered six-shooter.

It barely had time to clear leather when he was slammed back against the bar top, blood pouring from a hole in his chest. His mouth flapped open like a landed trout gasping for air as blood trickled from the wound. As life rapidly ebbed away, he collapsed in a heap on the floor.

That was the last that Nevado remembered.

Until now.


Once again Nevado peered at the marshal from beneath hooded eyebrows as it became clear what had happened next.

Cade willingly supplied the detail. His greying

moustache twitched in mirth.

'I was out back taking a leak when I heard everything go quiet as a graveyard. Now that ain't normal, I thinks to myself. Something's up. Quick as a flash,' – the lawman chuckled at his own wit – 'I fastened up and got back inside pronto. And there was you a-blasting some poor sap with that fancy hogleg.'

Nevado interrupted the marshal's lurid depiction with a venomous retort.

'So you snook up behind like some shifty polecat and slugged me.'

The leering smirk slipped from Cade's face. The whiskey-bloated snout twitched unconsciously, purpling even more than usual.

'It's lucky for you that I did, mister,' he railed, angrily slamming a bunched fist against the cell bars. 'I'd have been within my rights to gun you down afore that other skinner met the same fate as his partner. You oughta be damned grateful to me.'

'Yeh, Marshal,' replied the prisoner laying on the sarcasm with a thick trowel. 'I sure am grateful to have spent the night in this swanky establishment.'

But it went over Cade's head. He had skin as thick as a banker's wallet.

'And so you should be,' he said, shrugging, as he looked towards the heavy door leading to the office. 'Anyways, as I said before, you got visitors.'

Nevado frowned. He scratched his head. Nobody knew he was in this part of the country.

But then again, somebody obviously did.

'Who is it?' he asked, failing to hide the interest

13

plastered across his ashen features.

Cade responded with a snigger of disdain, but remained tight-lipped. Swinging on his heel, he returned to the outer office.

# TWO

# BOUGHT OFF

Two men were helping themselves from the coffee pot. One was over six feet in height with black greasy hair failing to hide the parchment-like skin drawn tight as a drumhead across an angular face. His partner was smaller, much more rounded and boasting a ruddy complexion, blotchy from an over-indulgence of bad whiskey.

Both were hard-bitten characters, so Cade decided to ignore the fact that they had also availed themselves of his best cigars. And judging by their dusty appearance, they had only recently hit town.

The unsavoury duo turned towards the marshal.

It was the taller of the two who spoke. He was clad in black leather even down to the tight-fitting gloves that encased his small hands like a second skin. It was obvious to the marshal that Jack Patch was in charge. The doubled-rigged gunbelt testified to that fact.

The other dude was merely there as back-up if needed. Mace Foggerty's rumpled brown suit had seen better days. His grizzled face and battered derby gave the impression of sluggish indolence. That said, the well-oiled Henry carbine cradled in his arms was not there for show. And the hard, beady eyes followed the marshal's every move.

'We heard in the saloon that you're holding a man with white hair,' stated Patch in a flat tone that gave nothing away. 'Is that right?'

'What's it to you?'

Cade had encountered rannies like these many times before. They smelt of trouble.

'What's he being held for?' added the man in black softly, ignoring the question and the lawman's terse attitude.

But Jubal Cade was not a man to be side-stepped.

'I'll ask you again, mister.' A brittle inflection had infiltrated the lawman's taut reply. 'What business do you have with my prisoner?'

Patch hesitated. His hackles rose, nerve ends tingling. He was not used to being challenged, even by a two-bit tin star like Cade. His natural reaction was to shoot first and to hell with the consequences. Nevertheless, he managed with an effort to stay cool. The boss had stressed that he wanted the man called Nevado, and that Patch should avoid trouble at all costs.

He stroked his jutting chin thoughtfully, keeping an eye on Jubal Cade from over the rim of his coffee mug. Mace Foggerty remained tight-lipped. He was

16

not a man of words. His talents were of the more lethal kind.

'I don't want any trouble, Marshal.' A loose smile cracked the taciturn demeanour as Patch tried to relax. He shrugged his narrow shoulders. 'It's just that my employer has need of this guy's particular talents.'

Despite his doubts regarding the duo's intentions, Cade was nonetheless intrigued. 'And what might those be?' he asked with rather less truculence. Still Patch chose to lead the verbal exchange.

'Mind if I take a look at this fella, Marshal?' he asked, already sidling across to the heavy oak door leading to the cell block.

'Be my guest.' Cade sensed that this tall sinister dude was playing with him, leading him by the nose. Nothing he could quite put his finger on, but the feeling made him edgy, tense. 'But first, shuck them hoglegs!'

Patch cracked an evil smile.

'Not taking any chances, are yuh, Marshal?'

'Damn right I ain't.'

'Can't say I blame yuh,' responded Patch, lifting his guns out of their fancy tooled rig and laying them on the marshal's desk. Then with a sly smirk he sauntered over to the cell block door.

Patch eyed the prisoner through the small barred aperture. He was not impressed. This was not the image he had expected to encounter. All the hired gunfighters he had previously come across were trail-hardened rannies, tough and ebullient. Men who

17

positively effused confidence. This sorry specimen was none of those things. Indeed, he looked more like the town drunk.

But the boss had insisted that the man with white hair was the best to fulfil the task he had in mind.

Nevado had come highly recommended by an associate of his from San Antonio. In addition to being a competent shootist, he was reputed to be one of that rare breed of gunfighters who could think on their feet.

Patch was not convinced. He signalled for Mace Foggerty to join him.

'What d'yuh reckon?' he asked, gesturing at the untidy heap splayed out on a bunk.

Foggerty handed his rifle to the marshal. On viewing the sprawled figure, he uttered a mirthless chortle, mean lips curling with contempt. A choice gob of chewing baccy was rolled around in his mouth and despatched with venom towards the recumbent form.

His aim was spot on.

'That's my opinion,' he spat.

'What the—!' Nevado lunged upright, clawing at the odious brown sludge trickling down his pasty cheeks.

Patch quickly noted the prisoner's automatic response was to grab for the missing gun on his hip, the natural reaction of any gunslinger backed into a corner. Maybe things were not all they seemed. And the boss had insisted this was the guy he wanted to hire.

Patch closed the small window shutter to block out the ranting curses issuing from the cell block and addressed his primary thought to the marshal.

'So what did this jigger do to get hisself locked up?'

Cade stoked up a fresh cigar, drew hard on the thin brown tube and proceeded to relate the events of the previous night.

Following the lawman's account, Patch strode over to the office window and gazed out on to the busy main street. His deliberations, however, were far removed from the comings and goings of the resident populace of Sonora.

'So what you aiming to do with him?' He threw the remark casually over his shoulder.

'Circuit judge is due in town at the end of the month,' replied Cade. 'He'll be given a fair trial. Then it's up to the judge to pass sentence. In view of the circumstances, I reckon a fine is all that will be imposed seeing as how the guy was provoked by them two skinners.'

'And what will you get out of this, Marshal?' Patch was thinking ahead. He tried to keep the strain out of his voice.

But Cade hadn't noticed. He shrugged nonchalantly.

'Usual arrest fee. Maybe a bit more if'n I can get that other skinner to testify that him and his partner had deliberately needled this turkey.' He slung a thumb towards the cellblock.

'Not much is it?' suggested Patch, eyeing the

19

lawdog closely.

'You ain't kiddin', mister.' A hint of discontent had invaded the lawman's tone. His voice became wistful, a dreamy cast playing around his pale eyes. 'Not like the old days when Jubal Cade was respected throughout Texas. Then I was the scourge of rustlers and road agents alike and could command any fee I asked for.' He shook his head sadly, clearly regretting the inevitable passage of time.

'Maybe I can help you out, Marshal,' offered Patch, a wry smile playing around the tight line of his mouth.

Suddenly Cade was all ears, if somewhat suspicious.

'How's that then?'

Patch hesitated, choosing his next words with care. The last thing he wanted now was to provoke any long dormant sense of rectitude in the ageing lawdog.

'What if I were to pay this guy's fine?' He paused then quickly added, 'Plus any fee that you reckon appropriate for the extra paperwork involved.' Patch took another breather, sucked hard on the rolled stogie then finished with, 'Not forgetting the inconvenience to your good self, of course.'

Cade's eyes lit up. He threw off the lethargy that had threatened to wash over him yet again, a fact of life that was happening more and more frequently these days. For five minutes he considered the proposal. The cigar rapidly disappeared in a cloud of blue smoke.

Jack Patch was left on tenterhooks.

'That ain't how the law works in Sonora,' he huffed some, whilst twiddling his moustache and trying to appear above reproach. 'I have a position to uphold that money can't buy.'

The lawman's apparent distaste at the suggestion was unconvincing. Patch could sense Cade's hesitance, the catch in his throat. The chance to earn extra dough was over-riding the lawman's sense of duty.

Patch pressed his argument. 'It's not as if this fella started the fracas, is it? If what you've told is right, he was only defending himself.'

Cade lit up a fresh cigar to aid his thinking. Taking a bottle of redeye from a drawer in his desk, he splashed a hefty measure into a glass and slung it down his gullet. The warm bite of the hard liquor helped steady his nerves. Then he announced purposefully, 'It'll cost you two hundred dollars . . . for the extra work involved.' Patch sucked in a deep breath.

'That's more'n I had in mind,' he wavered. His voice crackled with uncertainty. A helluva lot more. He had reckoned on no more than fifty. But returning to Buckeye empty-handed was unthinkable, a non-starter.

'OK,' he announced eventually with a sigh of resignation. Extracting a billfold from his jacket, he peeled off a wad of greenbacks.

'You sure about this, Jack?' queried a sceptical Mace Foggerty.

'Shut up!' growled Patch. 'You know what the boss said.'

Foggerty shrugged. He was just along for the ride: an extra gun in case of any unforseen emergency.

The marshal's eyes assumed an avaricious glint. He grabbed the cash and quickly counted the notes, stuffing them into his shirt pocket.

'Now if you will release the prisoner, Marshal,' hissed a waspish Jack Patch. 'We'll be on our way.'

'My pleasure, boys,' replied Cade exhuberantly. 'Good doing business with you.' The chuckle that followed caused Patch to fume inwardly, but he deemed it prudent to hold his peace.

Much to Nevado's surprise, he was unceremoniously ushered out of the cell block and his sixgun returned along with those of his benefactors.

An hour later, the unlikely trio were heading west out of Sonora.

Jack Patch led the way. He was followed by a puzzled Nevado with Foggerty bringing up the rear hauling a recalcitrant pack mule.

Nevado was pleased to have escaped the claustrophobic confines of the town's jailhouse. But his euphoria was soon replaced by unease as to what his two associates had in mind. He judged it wise to curb his burning curiosity. No doubt it would be satisfied in due course.

It was not until evening after they had made camp beside a chattering creek that his impatience finally wore thin.

They were well into the foothills of the Barrilla

Mountains. The three men were sitting around the flickering embers of a gutsy blaze, leaning easily against their saddles. Draped around their shoulders were blankets to stave off the chill wind that had blown up.

Nevado eyed the others closely, especially Jack Patch who was clearly the one in charge.

'Well?' he snapped. Akin to a whip crack, the sudden retort came out of the blue and was aimed at the man in black. 'What's this all about?'

Patch looked up, unexpectedly jerked from the hypnotic allure of the dancing flames.

'Ugh?' he grunted.

'Why did you pay off that starpacker in Sonora and get me off the hook?'

'All in good time, mister,' he replied casually, having regained his aplomb. 'You'll find out all you need to know when we reach Buckeye. The boss can be the one to fill you in seeing as how he's gonna be paying your wages.'

Nevado sucked in a deep breath of cold air, his body tense as a bridegroom on his wedding night.

'Either you spill the beans,' he hissed through clenched teeth, 'or I'm pulling out right now.'

He stood up and reached for his saddle.

The crackle of burning fire brands equally matched the tight atmosphere that had sprung up between the three men.

'You heard what the man said,' iterated Foggerty, his hand dropping to the holstered Smith & Wesson Schofield on his left hip. 'And you know what curiosity did, don't yuh?

Mace Foggerty reckoned himself to be a solid gunhand. That was his job. But he was no match for Nevado. Before he could even blink, the Frontier was palmed. It's silver barrel was jabbing unwaveringly at Foggerty's protruding belly before his own hand had even touched the pistol grip.

The hardcase was left staring, his fleshy mouth flapping like a hungry dogfish. Even Jack Patch was impressed. With some effort, he managed to maintain a cool indifference to the flashy display.

Nevado's face split in a grin colder than a mountain stream.

'Yep, I know all about curiosity,' he smirked lightly. 'Maybe it's you that's forgotten.'

At that moment, Jack Patch and Mace Foggerty could fully appreciate the reason why the boss had specifically wanted to hire the services of this white-haired gunfighter.

'So what's it to be?' pressed Nevado, jabbing the .44 to emphasize the fact that he would have no compunction in leaving if the two unlikely saviours were not forthcoming.

Foggerty let his hand fall away from the holstered pistol. He had no wish to go up against someone like Nevado. Glancing at his partner his piggy eyes rolled, informing Patch that it was his decision. Let him be the one to go against the boss's express order.

Patch relaxed visibly and sat down, gesturing for Nevado to do likewise. The tension eased as he nodded his concurrence that the gunfighter deserved to be put squarely in the picture.

# THREE

# EASY PICKINGS

Wade Garvey nudged his large bay to a gentle walk down the main street of the new town. Even beneath the thick layer of dust that caked his worn clothes, he was an imposing figure. Solid and unyielding, it was a look intended to warn off any troublemakers. Only those with an ardent death wish ever challenged the tough gang leader.

Black hair, now shot through with streaks of grey, emphasized the pitiless candour behind the dark brown eyes. Peering from beneath the wide brim of his Stetson like a hawk at chow time, nothing eluded the man's intensive gaze.

Beside him rode his trusted lieutenant, Jack Patch. An equally hard-nosed gunslinger. They had ridden together since the War and had come West after their last job had backfired. Garvey had always insisted his men wore red sashes tied around their thighs. He claimed it was for recognition when the lead started to fly. The notion had worked for the first few robberies they pulled back in their home state of Kansas.

But the Pinkertons had caught on. A large quantity of cash was advertised for shipment by the Kansas Pacific Railroad, and an ambush set to catch the 'Redlegs' when they attempted to rob the train. The ruse succeeded and half of Garvey's men were killed in the disastrous heist. As a result, the survivors were forced to flee the state.

That had been six months previously. During that time the red sashes had been abandoned and Garvey had managed to replace his losses with four new recruits. Mace Foggerty was one of these.

Garvey's orders were that they should always ride into any new settlement in pairs to avoid drawing unnecessary attention to themselves. And red was banned, even down to their underwear.

Pickings had been slim since the gang had left Kansas. But Wade Garvey still exuded a tough persona that brooked no dissent. His confident manner suggested that things would improve once they left civilization behind.

But he was more than a little aware of his own limitations. Well into middle age, train and bank robberies no longer held the excitement they had in the first flush of his youth. That sort of illicit activity was proving far too dangerous for a man in his mid-forties. If he intended to welcome in his fiftieth birthday, Garvey needed a less traumatic, yet more lucrative source of income.

His idea was to find someplace where the pickings were much easier: a place on the edge of the frontier far removed from the all-seeing eye of the Pinkerton Detective Agency.

Buckeye looked just right.

Located in the remote outlands of West Texas, it appeared at first glance to have everything of which a scheming outlaw like Wade Garvey could take full advantage. There were a lot of new buildings being erected, including some of brick which indicated that this was no fly-by-night boom town.

Old habits found him searching out the most important. A bank always indicated there was money in the locality. Even more enlightening with regard to Buckeye was the fact that a second one was in the course of being constructed.

Garvey nodded approvingly.

Yessiree! This could be his lucky break.

Only one fly in the ointment that he could see.

The unwelcome sign bearing the appendage: *Town Marshal* could be seen flapping idly in the fetid air halfway down the dusty street on the left-hand side. And there was said official, lounging in a chair outside his office puffing contentedly on an old corn cob.

Garvey's mouth parted in a cruel, thin-lipped smile. He nudged his partner, indicating the old dude who was clearly just seeing out his time until retirement. Well that would come sooner than he expected. A nice little accident in due course and Garvey could install his own man to protect the town's interests, not to mention his own.

Swivelling round in the high cantle of the Mexican saddle, he surveyed his back trail. As expected, two of his men were waiting under the shadowed overhang of a cottonwood on the edge of town. The rest of the gang would arrive in Buckeye after dark.

Even from this distance, Ace Montana was unmistakable, the tell-tale ace of diamonds sticking out of his hat band. Being a gambler of no mean repute, Montana liked to advertise his profession in a flamboyant manner.

His partner was a new boy whom Garvey had picked up whilst passing through Amarillo. Mace Foggerty had come to Montana's aid when a skulking backshooter had tried to terminate the gambler's career during a rigged poker game. It had meant a swift exit from the town with hot lead chasing their tails. The gang boss, ever on the lookout for dexterous gunhands, had invited Foggerty to join them.

Nevado was becoming impatient. He toed the glowing embers of the fire. They spluttered and cackled in protest.

'I ain't asking for a history lesson,' he spat with a reproving look. 'So how about you boys getting down to the nitty gritty of this confab.'

'Just puttin' you in the picture, is all,' replied Patch, ignoring the barbed retort. 'It's best that you know what this is all about and the sort of fella you'll be workin' fer.' He paused, mean eyes narrowed to thin slits as he carefully appraised the gunfighter, attempting to probe beneath the pokerfaced expression before continuing. 'Can I take it you ain't averse to bendin' the law a little?'

Nevado returned the penetrating gaze.

'Depends how far. I sure wouldn't want it to break up and smack me in the kisser.' In response, a brief smile played across the outlaw's craggy features before Nevado went on. 'And naturally, I would expect a bonus in my pay packet when the job has been completed.'

'I reckon the boss wouldn't quibble with that,' replied Patch easily. 'So long as he ain't implicated in any way.'

A silence descended over the tiny pool of light surrounding the campsite. Mace Foggerty had retreated to the outer shadows, a ghostly figure watching the state of play as his partner resumed the narrative. Nevado had noted the surreptitious manoeuvre. These guys were no greenhorn rough riders. Still, that had to be a good thing: he hated working with dead wood.

Inside of six months, Wade Garvey had made his presence well and truly felt in Buckeye. His own man was firmly established in the marshal's office and the town council were eating out of his hand, thanks to monthly backhanders.

Regular income came in the form of protection fees demanded of the local storekeepers. In the beginning, a couple had balked at the notion of paying up when they already had the law to protect them. Of course, it was merely a coincidence when accidental fires had destroyed their livelihoods. The others soon took the hint and fell into line.

He and his men had taken over the upper floor of the Texas Belle saloon, and were enjoying the fruits of their nefarious activities. Within three months, Garvey was in full control of the establishment.

Everything should have been rosy in the garden.

Patch took a deep breath and emitted a sombre grunt. He reached for a burning twig and relit his cigar before resuming. As if in accord, the evening breeze rustled the leaves of a clutch of dwarf willows.

Nevado instantly picked up on the guy's nervous inflection. Now they were really getting to the crux of the matter.

'Things were going along smoothly as far as we were concerned,' declared Patch. 'Then it happened. . . .' Beads of sweat broke out on his forehead, reflected in the firelight like macabre dancing devils.

'What happened?' Nevado was caught up in the tense narration now that it had reached the critical stage.

'Guys started disappearing. First off it was Brad Salter, then One-Eyed Tab Sinclair.' Patch shook his head as he recalled the bizarre chain of events. 'We couldn't figure it out. Wade was real sore. Thought they'd just lit out for pastures new without sayin' a word. But that theory took a tumble when we found all their gear still in their rooms. Nobody hits the trail empty-handed, do they?'

He didn't wait for a response.

'The crunch came when the bodies were found accidentally by a hunter in a box canyon some five miles out of town.' Patch gulped uneasily casting a twitching peeper towards his white-haired companion. 'Both of 'em had had their throats cut, slit open from ear to ear like pigs on a butcher's slab.'

Mace Foggerty had emerged from the gloom, drawn by the menacing turn in the dialogue.

'I've seen some grim sights in my time,' he muttered, the words trembling with a marked trepidation alien to his character. 'But when the third body turned up. . . .' The gunman paced up and down sucking hard on a quirly to calm his frazzled nerve ends.

There was no further need to embroider the account. Nevado was now in the picture and fully aware of why he was heading for Buckeye with these two hard-nosed but equally fearful outlaws.

Wade Garvey was clearly out of his depth. He desperately needed someone to find the killer of his men before any more suffered a similar fate at the hands of the demon knife-wielder.

'Are you interested then?' enquired Patch tentatively.

Nevado allowed himself the hint of a smile. This could prove to be a lucrative assignment.

'How much is Garvey paying?' he asked.

'He mentioned a grand.' Instantly reading the disdain etched across the gunfighter's rugged features, Patch hurried on to reassure him. 'But I reckon you could name your price to rid us of this bastard.'

'Things that bad, eh?'

Interesting, thought Nevado, very interesting. An outlaw stuck between a rock and a hard place: now that was a new one.

# FOUR

## WADE GARVEY

It was four days later when the three riders finally crested Black Mesa overlooking a broad valley some ten miles wide. They drew rein and contemplated the terrain marking the end of their journey. For his two companions, it was a reminder of their own precarious situation.

But for Nevado, it was a new beginning. An opportunity to make himself a hefty wedge and ensure his future. A smile of satisfaction greeted the notion.

Buckeye was located on a terrace where the tributary flow of the Salt Draw forked in to the mighty Pecos River. Although the land appeared to be parched and dry, Nevado could see cattle dotted across the expansive range. They were in the process of being rounded-up in preparation for the long drive to the northern railheads.

It would appear that Buckeye was the focus of the West Texas cattle industry, and as such a prosperous

33

town with a secure future. He could readily understand why Wade Garvey had chosen it for his
perverse activities.

Still, that was none of his concern. He had a job to
do. And he was determined that the gang boss was
going to make his trip West an equally profitable
venture.

Jogging down the shallow grade, the three riders
merged into a rutted trail and were soon entering
the outer limits of the town. On the surface, there
appeared to be nothing out of the ordinary. Folks
were going about their everyday business; wagons
were being loaded up with supplies for the local
ranches.

New houses being constructed on the edge of
town were clearly for the wealthier citizens. Passing
the junction signposted Nob Hill, they stretched up
a shallow gradient. At the top stood a garishly
opulent mansion. Nevado idly wondered if his future
employer had commissioned a similar one.

As they turned into Main Street, he couldn't help
noticing that his sidekicks were receiving hostile if
rather furtive glances. Could these be the citizens
who were having to pay for protection? More than
likely.

He shrugged off the discordant thought. None of
his concern.

Jack Patch jabbed a finger towards a large building
some fifty yards up on the right.

'The Texas Belle!' he announced proudly. 'The
best place in town. And we occupy the whole of the

first floor. You'll have Mooney's old room.'

Nevado's brow creased in a quizzical frown.

'And what happened to Mooney?' he enquired idly.

Patch's mouth tightened. his swarthy features assuming a waxy pallor. The reply, when it came, emerged as a flat monotone.

'He's one of the reason's you're here.'

'Oh, right,' said Nevado catching the drift. 'You never mentioned him. I shoulda guessed.'

'Lex Mooney was the last buzzard to split the breeze.'

Patch shook his head as the whole bizarre chain of recent events smacked him in the mouth. Desperately, he tried to shake off the dull ache that was twisting at his guts. The last thing he needed was to display any sign of fear in front of Nevado. Patch had himself attempted a change of career by suggesting to Garvey that he could soon bring the killer to book, although he pointedly refrained from disclosing this fact to his new associate.

It had not proved to be a successful claim.

Quickly reaffirming his normal cocksure persona, the outlaw hurried on, a blustering grin daubed across the pallid exterior. 'You'll be pleased to know that it's right next door to my room. That way I can make sure you settle in, comfortable like.'

Nevado knew that the real reason was so that Patch could keep an eye open for his boss's investment. He met the gunman's hard grimace with an angled measure of disdain.

Both men knew where they stood.

Tying up outside the grandiose building with its lavishly baroque portico, Patch led the way inside. Even in the middle of the day, the saloon was doing a roaring trade.

Cowboys off the range mingled with carpetbaggers and tarted-up lost doves plying their age-old profession. A card game was in progress to his left. Nevado recognized Ace Montana instantly from his ostentatious bearing. Over in the corner, a trio of musicians was banging out a jaunty number to which various couples were jigging merrily.

The hired gunnie couldn't help eliciting a surprised murmur when, just like the waters of the Red Sea, the chaotic mêlée parted to allow the recently arrived trio unimpeded access to the staircase at the far end of the large room. Nevado was impressed. Garvey and his gunhands certainly appeared to have established more than a modicum of leverage on the saloon's clientele.

The raucous babble was instantly muted. Even the music stumbled to a discordant halt as Patch and his sidekick swaggered down the middle of the room. Like strutting peacocks, they were revelling in the notoriety.

Nevado was more circumspect. He was delving into unknown territory here, and, as such, it paid to err on the side of discretion.

Only when the three men had disappeared from view along the top corridor did the level of displaced noise reassert itself, although now somewhat moderated as the general source of conversation turned to speculating on the presence of the mysterious white-haired stranger.

Patch knocked on the door at the end of the corridor.

'Who is it?' came back the brusque retort.

'It's Jack, boss,' called out the gunman through the closed door. 'I got Mace with me. We've brought in that fella you sent us after – the white-haired gunfighter, calls hisself Nevado.'

Following a brief murmur of subdued voices from the far side of the door, it was quickly opened and a scowling face appeared bearing more creases than an ageing bloodhound. More significant, however, was the cocked double-gauge Greener aimed at the newcomers.

Nevado couldn't resist allowing a cagey smirk to bend his lip. Garvey was obviously rattled, and taking no chances.

On seeing that it was indeed his henchmen, the gang boss beckoned them into the room whilst the hard-nosed minder resumed his stance by the door, shotgun clutched grimly across his chest. He was a half-breed Indian and went under the handle of Choctaw Pete.

Three other hard-nosed villains slouched against the wall, coolly appraising the white-haired gunfighter. Looks of arrogant disregard couldn't disguise the inherent curiosity and uncertainty the arrival of this hired trouble-shooter had engendered in them all.

Everybody knew why he was here. It hadn't gone down well that the boss had seen fit to look outside his own ranks for a solution the deadly predicament they all now faced.

Nevado brazenly scrutinized the gang boss sitting on the far side of a wide, leather-topped desk, ostensibly studying some papers. A garishly embroidered brocade vest contrasted with the sober cut of his expensive, tailor-made blue suit. And judging by his bulging waistline, Wade Garvey was assuredly enjoying the trappings of his new-found source of income. Trying to appear the affluent businessman, he sported a heavily waxed moustache, one end of which he was absent-mindedly twirling.

Eventually the gang boss laid aside a gold-plated pen and deigned to acknowledge the presence of the newcomer.

Nevado held his gaze with a flat stare, cool and unflinching.

Standing up, Garvey reached into his jacket pocket and extracted two cigars. Still eyeing the hired gun with a steady assessment, he handed one to Nevado and gestured for him to be seated.

One of the lounging gunmen immediately struck a vesta and applied the sputtering flame to his chief's cigar. He finished by blowing it out and insolently flicking the spent taper at the unwelcome visitor.

Garvey uttered a rancid growl.

'What about Mr Nevado then?'

The arrogant leer instantly faded from the thug's oily face as he hurried to obey, suitably browbeaten.

'S-sorry, boss.'

Both men ignored the apology, puffing easily on their smokes.

'So Mr Nevado,' began Garvey leaning back in his chair. 'I trust you had a pleasant—'

'Just Nevado!' interrupted the gunfighter. 'And let's cut out the small talk. We all know I ain't here for a vacation.'

Garvey nodded. 'As you wish . . . Nevado.' There was a deliberate pause before he continued. 'Straight down to business. Just what I like. You are indeed a man after my own heart, Nevado.' Another hefty pull on the cigar. 'I'm glad that my boys' managed to find you. And persuade you to accompany them back to Buckeye. Did they tell you anything about the little . . . er, shall we say . . . difficulty that we are facing here?'

Nevado uttered a harsh chuckle. 'You might want to call it a difficulty,' he said. 'Far as I can see, this is one helluva fix you're in, mister.' Nevado deliberately drew hard on his cigar relishing the taste of the expensive Havana before adding, 'In fact, I'd say you were in deep shit, and I intend setting my fee accordingly.'

The false affability dissolved from Garvey's graven image to be replaced by a blunt regard.

'So what have you in mind?' he hissed, gripping the arms of his chair so that the knuckles blanched whiter that Nevado's thatch.

Again, the gunfighter fixed a jaundiced eye on the gang boss.

'Five grand! Half now, the rest when I. . . .' – now it was Nevado's turn to play the hesitation ploy – 'locate and dispose of the problem.'

Garvey spluttered, his face turning a virulent puce as he struggled to control his temper. He had figured on no more than a thousand. His threatening gaze shifted to Jack Patch. The gunman's face assumed a russet hue, but he remained silent.

'What?' Garvey exclaimed, slamming a tight-balled fist down on his desk. A glass of whiskey jumped in the air, as did the other occupants in the room. All except Nevado, who remained seated, cool as the north wind.

'You heard,' he said quietly. 'No haggling. You want the best, you pay for it. And believe me when I tell you: I am the best.' He fixed a hard stare on the gang boss. It paid to exude boundless confidence in this game. 'So, what's it to be?'

Garvey's black eyes bore deep into the man sitting opposite.

'Nobody dictates to Wade Garvey,' he snarled. 'Patch told you I'd pay a grand for this job. If'n you didn't like it, why did you come all this way?' A sneering hint of bravado lent emphasis to the prodding finger. 'Any one of my boys could take you out right now. And nobody in this town would lift a finger to find the killer.'

Nevado shook his head, uttering a manic chortle. His large eyes glinted with scornful derision. 'Do you really think I'm that stupid?' he hollered. 'Entering the lion's den without some kinda backup. Right now, there's a derringer aimed at your black heart. You'd be dead afore any of these turkeys could slap leather. And if you don't believe me, ask Jack or Mace here.'

Garvey turned to his henchmen.

'He sure is one mean gunsel, boss,' averred Patch, with grudging respect.

'I wouldn't go up agin' him,' agreed Foggerty nodding vigorously.

'And another thing,' cut in Nevado forcefully. 'If I walk outa here, you'll still be in the same position you are now, but the hole would be that much deeper. Next time it could be one of these jiggers spilling his guts into the river.'

Slowly, like a slinky mountain lion, he eased himself up off the chair and turned to leave before continuing, 'Or maybe even yourself.' Broad shoulders lifted in a shrug of indifference. 'But if that's your answer, I'll be on my way.'

The office door opened.

'Wait!' shouted Garvey, wiping a smear of moisture from his lower lip. 'Perhaps I was a mite hasty. It's all this business of losing my boys to some unknown bushwhacker that's gettin' me down. It's enough to send any man insane.'

He motioned for Nevado to resume his seat.

'So you agree to my terms?'

Garvey realized that he had little choice in the matter. He could certainly raise the money. And if he refused? It didn't bear thinking on. He would be forced to leave Buckeye, tail between his legs. Such an ignominious retreat would be the end of the line for Wade Garvey. His reputation would be shattered. He would then become the target for any young gun on the prod.

'OK, I agree.' Accompanied by a curt nod, the response was cowed. But issued with a taut adjunct. 'Just get the job done, and darned quickly too.'

Nevado's response was an exaggerated salute.

'You're the boss. I'll get started just as soon as that down payment is sitting in my account at the hank.'

'First thing in the morning,' complied Garvey.

Nevado moved to the door, his every movement pursued by truculent looks that were nevertheless impotent. He had the whip hand and knew it.

Before leaving, he swung on his heel addressing his remark to the subdued gang boss. 'If'n you want me for anything in the meantime, I'll be staying at the Imperial Hotel.' He laid a trenchant eye on Jack Patch, smiling at the uneasy reaction as he continued, 'I get a might tetchy with people looking over my shoulder. It'll be on my expenses sheet.'

Without waiting for a reply, he slammed the door shut and went down to the bar to begin marking up that said sheet. And it sure wouldn't be the normal rotgut they dished up in most saloon bars.

Nosirree! Only the best for Nevado from now on. A broad grin split the normally taciturn features. He was going to enjoy this job.

# FIVE

# A GRIM DISCOVERY

The arrival of Nevado and his two chaperons had not gone unnoticed, nor unheeded. Aaron Spedding always kept a close eye on any newcomers who hit town. But he had paused overlong in his perusal of the tall white-haired stranger hauling rein outside the Texas Belle. It was the waspish demand for attention from a half-lathered client in the midst of a shave who brought him down to earth with a bump.

'You gonna stare out that window all day, Aaron?'

'S-sorry about that, Homer,' he opined apologetically whilst vigorously stropping a razor. 'Just being nosy as usual.' A tight laugh obligingly concealed his fazed demeanour. The last thing he wanted was to draw unwelcome attention to his interest in the comings and going of Wade Garvey's bunch of hard-cases. 'Barbers always like to sniff out any new business.'

Homer Radcliffe grunted. All he was interested in

was picking up his monthly order from the feed merchant and getting back to his ranch. The other customers awaiting their turn in the barber's chair thankfully hadn't noticed anything untoward.

The barber was a little on the short side, with rather less hair on his bullet head than he would have liked. What little had survived his twenty-seven years was plastered down with the potent allure of a thick pomade. There was even less on his smoothly aquiline face. On the other hand, Aaron was a meticulous dresser who always insisted on wearing a clean white shirt each day accompanied by a different neck tie. It afforded his customers a talking point, a facet to his work that Spedding liked to encourage.

Some two hours later when he was about to shut up shop for the day, he again noticed the stranger emerging from the saloon. On this occasion, the guy was accorded more than a passing glance. It was obvious that he was no ordinary saddle tramp. As the only barber in town, Aaron dealt with all manner of individuals whilst attending to their bodily needs. And, as such, he had become an astute observer, a finely honed judge of human nature in all its singular peculiarities.

A knowing bob of the head followed. Here was a earnest gunfighter if ever there was one, and definitely above the normal calibre that Garvey kept on his payroll. That was clear from his bearing. Not even the shabby trail gear could hide the fact that this jigger could wipe the floor with any of the hicks inhabiting the Texas Belle, even Jack Patch.

The barber's smoothly domed brow wrinkled in thought. There was one question that he could not answer. What business did such a fellow have with a low life of Wade Garvey's ilk?

There was only one way to find out.

Ignoring the loose hair that required sweeping up, he donned his jacket and hurried over to the Texas Belle. Peering down the street, his beady peepers noted the stranger entering the hallowed precincts of the Imperial Hotel.

A mindful smirk creased the soft features. He had been right in his assumptions. Only those with influence or a thick billfold graced the portals of such a high-class establishment.

Miss Penelope Wilson saw to that. The manageress had arrived in Buckeye three months ago and had immediately seen the potential for a high class hotel. The rundown premises had been quickly transformed into the thriving establishment it had now become.

Unobtrusively, the barber entered the saloon, his manner circumspect and decidedly nervous. The clear indication of this being Wade Garvey's territory became instantly apparent as wary eyes panned the smoke-filled room. In addition to the usual clientele, Garvey minders idly whiled away their time playing the tables or chatting up the array of girls on offer. This while attempting to guard their boss's back.

Spedding couldn't resist a silent chuckle. If only they knew. The notion, however, dispensed an icy shiver through his corpulent frame. Stepping up to the bar he ordered a small beer.

'Don't often see you in here, Aaron,' announced the bartender pushing the frothing glass across the shiny bar top.

The barber was well known to all the male citizens. And popular too as he always gave a good service. He was also a good listener, lending a sympathetic ear to all manner of domestic complaints, grumbles and disputes, none of which went beyond the walls of the barber's shop. People felt they could trust the little fat man. After all, what threat was he to any of them? This was what Aaron Spedding was counting on.

'Figured I've earned a drink,' he replied, thinking as to how he might broach the subject of the white-haired stranger. 'It's been a busy day.'

'And mighty hot as well,' added the barman, joining his customer in a drink. 'A cold beer slides down a treat and no mistake.'

'Sure does.'

Aaron coughed to hide his jumpiness. He needed to make this sound like a general query, of no importance.

'Strange fella passed me outside just now,' he began, pausing to take a drink whilst watching the barman for his reaction. 'Maybe you know him.'

'Who was that then?'

'Tall jasper with thick white hair.'

The barman's eyes widened.

Aaron sucked in his breath. He obviously knew the dude to whom the barber was referring. The little man waited for the dubious frown, the snarled response for the barber to mind his own business.

Spedding hurried on, hoping to allay any suspicion that he might harbour an ulterior motive in the enquiry.

'That mop could do with a good trim and styling if'n you ask me.'

The barman nodded in agreement. Aaron breathed a sigh of relief when he perceived that the man's reaction bore no skepticism. Instead, he leaned across the bar and replied in lowered tones intended for no other ears.

'The boss has brought him in to help find the bastard what's getting rid of his henchmen. He's rattled I can tell yuh.'

Aaron hung on his every word. Elation at this announcement was tempered by a jolt of alarm that some professional gunslinger had been hired to hunt down the killer. Aaron struggled to contain any display of feelings communicating itself to his ruddy complexion.

'What's his name?' The question emerged as a hoarse croak.

'Calls hisself Nevado. Apparently it means snow white in Spanish. He's from Amarillo.' The barman pulled Aaron another beer, brushing aside the offer of payment. 'My guess is he'll be charging a hefty fee for his services.'

'I can understand that,' the barber concurred with a shrewd grimace. Injecting a note of serious concern into his voice he replied, 'Just seen him disappearing into the Imperial.'

'Mighta guessed,' agreed the barman. 'Nobody stays in that swell joint unless they're particularly well heeled.'

Downing the beer, Aaron nodded, assiduously thanking the barman for his generosity. He deemed it sensible to omit that his gratitude was really for the information unwittingly imparted rather than the free drink. Then he made his excuses and left, fully satisfied that his visit to the Texas Belle had been time well spent.

Back in his little shop, Aaron Spedding slumped into one of his upright chairs. The mess on the floor went unheeded, the empty bottles of lotion unfilled. This latest development needed thinking on.

Staring deep into his mirrored reflection, an uncharacteristic glare peered back. No longer the slack-jawed, flabby scissorman who fussed and preened over which aromatic unction his customer would suit best, here was presented the authentic Aaron Spedding. Stripped down to the bare bones, it was a brutally threatening image to which nobody else could ever be a witness.

Silently and alone, he contemplated the circumstances that had brought him to his present situation. The remembrance was profoundly hurtful.

Long fingernails dug hard into the soft palms of his hands drawing a thin trickle of blood. The pain went unheeded.

Aaron's thoughts drifted back twelve years to that awful day when his well-ordered life had been torn apart. The horrendous scream was as real now as it ever was. Like an animal thrashing in its death throes, the chilling sound was not of this world. Yet it was coming from the farmhouse where he had been born, and lived happily for the last fifteen years.

His mother had died two years previously of the fever, so it had to be his sister. But what sort of dire shock could have elicited such an unearthly shriek of the most despicable agony? Even at that distance, the abhorrent nature of the bestial utterance had cut through the static air like a knife though butter.

Dropping the pitchfork which he had been using to pile up the hay crop, Aaron began running for all he was worth back towards the farm. He had covered half the distance when three shots punched the air, one after the other, instantly halting the racing youth in his tracks.

A final throaty gurgle followed.

Then silence.

Aaron stood in the middle of the unharvested field of corn. Arms by his side, he found himself incapable of movement, riveted to the spot and unable to comprehend the enormity of the situation that had been thrust into his naïve young mind.

Almost immediately, another more normal sound assailed his senses.

The drumming of hoofs soon resolved itself into a group of horsemen. They swung into sight appearing to be in no hurry. Trotting in single file out of the farmyard and around the end of the barn, they headed down the access track led by a large man sporting a heavy black beard.

Aaron automatically ducked down below the level of the grain crop. He could clearly observe the riders approaching but was effectively concealed by the billowing ocean of ripening corn. When they came opposite his hideout, the gang leader signalled a halt. Stepping down from the saddle he proceeded to tighten a loose cinch.

Assuming they were alone, the blackguard unwittingly revealed his face to the terrified youngster who was crouched no more than ten feet away. Beneath the beard, a brutal visage seemed to be gazing right into Aaron's very soul. The boy held his breath, fearful that the slightest sound would reveal his presence.

The big man turned away, his features lost in shadow. But not before Aaron had caught sight of the livid scar gouged across his ugly kisser. A malign white snake connecting the corner of his mouth to his right ear.

'Where we headed now, boss?' came the shouted query from one of the riders. 'We can't stick around Grant's County with them bodies litterin' the place. The law'll be on to us in the flick of a rattler's tongue.'

'Good job we managed to persuade the old bastard to cough up his savings,' chortled another. 'At least we've gotten some'n outa this fracas.'

'Jack sure came away with a smile on his kisser.'

'You said it, Colorado. That little gal sure hit the right spot.' The odious comment from another hardcase evoked a loathsome rumble of laughter from the rest of the group.

'Pity she wasn't so agreeable to your pawing, wouldn't yuh say, Jack?'

The man addressed as Jack winced as he fingered the twin nail gashes clearly etched on his left cheek like railroad tracks.

'She paid the price.'

The frigidly sneering remark was accompanied by a meaningful tap on the sheathed bowie knife on his hip. It was this revelation that brought Aaron out of his stupor. He almost jumped out of hiding to challenge the cold-blooded outlaw.

In the nick of time, he held himself in check. With no weapon handy, he stood to end up with lead poisoning like his pa or skewered on that lethal blade like his sister.

'Enough of this caterwaulin',' hissed the gang leader gruffly, settling himself easily in the saddle. 'We've still got that little job I planned down in Springfield. Wade Garvey ain't afeared of no goddamned tin star.' He set his hat straight, digging the lethal Spanish rowels viciously into the horse's flanks. Then with a final flourish he trilled, 'Once that's over, we can leave this mangy state behind and head for Texas.'

Those were the last words of the detestable killer that Aaron heard as the gang disappeared in a cloud of dust.

But they were enough.

*Wade Garvey!* and a skunk by the name of *Jack*.

The hated names and that heinously scarred face were branded forever on to Aaron's brain. Someday he would track the bastard down and extract the full penalty in retribution.

It was early evening before the boy finally plucked up the nerve to return to the farmhouse. Sheer exhaustion had taken control of mind and body causing him to fall asleep involuntarilly in the cornfield.

When he finally awoke, lengthening shadows were cutting a swathe across the serene landscape. In the west, the golden orb dipped low towards the far line of hills offering an idyllic tableau that passed unnoticed as the youngster slowly dragged his protesting feet across the farmyard. The first thing he saw was the blooded corpse of his father splayed out at an obscene angle in the doorway of the house.

A buzzard perched on the hitch rail eagerly anticipating its supper.

The sight of the hungry predator launched a stomach-churning howl of anguish from the boy. Arms waving like a demented scarecrow, he rushed across the intervening few yards. The bird flapped away out of range emitting a disconsolate series of squawks.

His father's waxy features were fixed in a terror-stricken rictus too awful to contemplate. Aaron quickly removed his coat and placed it over the bullet-riddled torso. Gingerly he stepped around the body and pushed open the sagging door peering inside the rapidly darkening living-room.

Initially he could see nothing.

As his eyes adjusted to the gloom, the true nature of what had occurred struck home like a stampeding herd of angry longhorns. Though acutely aware of the untold agonies that Sarah must have suffered after being so savagely violated, Aaron couldn't remove his horrified gaze from the naked body of his older sister.

The reality was far worse than even his darkest imaginings had envisaged. Powerless to look away, he stood there, rigidly transfixed to the spot.

It was the renewed bout of greed-induced cawing from outside that jolted him back to the reality of his situation.

A blanket was quickly sought to assuage his guilty conscience.

Unable to remain in the house any longer, Aaron spent a fitful night in the barn. What sleep he could manage eventually arrived in the early hours, although scathingly punctuated by virulent night-mares. It was the crowing of the farm rooster that eventually brought him to wakefulness, screeching in terror as the horrific events were replayed in his tortured subconscious.

Father and sister were buried in a shady plot behind the house. No prayers were said over the unmarked graves. Aaron had effectively forsaken any notions of belief in a forgiving deity.

All he could now think about was revenge. The need to inscribe his own brand of justice on the perpetrators of this heinous crime against his family tore at his innards. What form that would take he had no way of estimating.

Next day, Aaron abandoned the farmstead. It was only rented so he had nothing to lose. Apart from his horse, all he took with him was a change of clothes and what provisions he was able to stuff into a gunny sack. Knowing the gang were headed for Springfield in his native Missouri at least gave him an initial destination.

He had no idea how he was going to confront the gang when he got there, nor indeed how he was going to make his own way in life.

But ignorance is bliss to an ingenuous fifteen-year-old who assumed that everything would fall into place.

After three days on the trail with his provisions running low, the grim reality of the task he had set himself began to impinge itself on his naive young mind. And Springfield was still more than a week's ride away.

Then his horse threw a shoe.

But Aaron Spedding was determined that vengeance would be exacted.

It would be a long time coming.

# SIX

## NO PUSHOVER

Opening his eyes, Aaron once again gazed at the drawn features in the mirror. He shook his head trying to shake off the woolly cloak that encased his brain. Unwittingly, his hand must have found the bottle of whiskey he kept nearby for favoured customers. It had been full. Now it was almost empty. Blotchy red patches on his face contrasted with the dark rings under the watery eyes.

Nobody had realized that the innocuous barber was a drinking man. Just one more secret he kept locked away.

Life had not treated him kindly in other ways. What little hair he had left was a lifeless grey, a fact which made him look far older than his years.

Not being one of the hard-bitten rannies who normally inhabited frontier towns, Aaron had survived by talking his way out of trouble and living on his wits. Barbering had come naturally to the young man. And he had quickly discovered that even the most gun-crazy roustabouts enjoyed a little attentive pampering.

But of Wade Garvey and his men, there had been no sign. They appeared to have vanished off the face of the earth. Occasional snippets of information had found him upping sticks and heading off on forays that had all proved to be wild goose chases.

The years passed with no firm sightings. Was the killer even still alive? Maybe he had been caught, tried and convicted. Aaron hoped not, because he wanted to be judge, jury and executioner.

After twelve years of fruitless searching, he had arrived in Buckeye.

Just another town on his endless quest. But it had no barber. Maybe he could settle down here for a spell.

It was only a matter of days after he had opened up the new premises for business that he received a visit from a pair of hard-nosed varmints. As soon as they entered the shop Aaron smelt trouble.

Silence engulfed the other three customers who each nervously made a vague excuse about having to be elsewhere.

'Can I help you, gentlemen?' intoned the barber pasting a forced smile on to his soft visage.

One of them, a half-caste Indian sporting a large eagle feather in his hat, silently closed the door and put the closed sign up. Dressed in black from head to toe, the other dude was clearly the spokesman.

'I figure it's us that can help you, barber,' he hissed

while lighting up a cigar.

'You are wanting a haircut?'

Silence. The query merely elicited a mirthless grin from the hardcase.

'Bath and manicure maybe?'

'You didn't hear right, mister. I said we're the ones offering the help.'

'And what help might that be?' replied Aaron, beginning to feel decidedly jittery. 'Are you after selling hair tonic? Or shaving cream?'

The man in black emitted a high-pitched cackle.

'You sure are one funny guy, barber.' The ugly laugh faded away as quickly as it had erupted. Black eyes gushing pure menace narrowed to thin slits, the cruel mouth curling in a brittle sneer. 'Maybe too funny.'

'I can assure you, sir,' said Aaron, with a disposition that strongly hinted of the growing sense of disquiet he could barely conceal. His legs felt like jelly. 'I will certainly assist you any way I can, if it is within my power.'

'That's better,' smirked the mean-eyed visitor. 'I knew you'd come round to my way of thinkin' in the end. This fella's got sense, ain't he, Choctaw?'

The half-breed merely grunted.

Aaron waited, nervously expectant. A film of sweat glistened on his high forehead. Outside, a heavy clap of thunder heralded a storm in the making. It was not an auspicious omen.

'My boss reckons you're in need of an insurance policy.' The man removed an official-looking form from inside his jacket. 'It'll only cost you twenty bucks a month. Cheap at the price if'n you ask me. Just sign on the dotted line and we'll be on our way.'

The barber's mouth dropped a fraction as he peered through his round spectacles at the form, then back at the smirking salesman. Now he knew what this was all about: a protection racket!

Well he was having none of it.

The beady eyes hardened to chilly lumps of ice, the fleshy jaw tightening as Aaron Spedding attempted to draw himself up to his full height. It was not an action likely to impress the strutting critter.

Nor did it.

'You aren't gonna prove awkward, I hope?' he cut back. The words crackled with willful menace.

'I already have all the insurance I need, thank you,' Aaron replied curtly. He turned away and began tidying up. 'Now if you wouldn't mind, I'm closing.'

He failed to witness the brief look that passed between the pair of toughs. The crash that followed was meant to shock, and it most assuredly succeeded.

Aaron jumped. Flinching involuntarily, he swung round to see his mirror lying in pieces, jagged shards of glass embedded in one of the barbering chairs. The half-breed slowly handed his smoking shotgun to his sidekick then picked up a large jar of green lotion. Squinting in oblivious ignorance at the label, he then deliberately hurled it at the wall. The jar shattered into a myriad pieces, its contents spilling across the salon.

An inane grin pasted on to the Indian's weathered

contours informed Aaron that this was a game he was enjoying immensely. Selecting another container, it was only the raised hand of his associate that prevented further damage.

'That's enough, Choctaw.' The evil grimace held no trace of humour. 'For now, anyway. We'll be back tomorrow when I'm sure Mr Spedding will be only too eager to co-operate. After all, we're only thinkin' of his best interests, ain't we?'

The question required no response, and received none.

With that explicit threat hanging in the air and a final chilling guffaw, the man squared his shoulders and left with his partner. The door slammed hard shut behind them, dislodging some loose fragments of glass.

Aaron slumped into a vacant chair. His heart was pumping like a runaway locomotive, breath rasping harshly in his dry throat.

It was some hours later that night after he had finally cleared up the mess that anger set in with a vengeance. Fear and the threat to life and limb had receded in the company of a few tumblers of whiskey. He determined that no jumped-up tricksters were going to cheat Aaron Spedding out of his livelihood. First thing on the morrow, he would go round to the Texas Belle and make a vociferous complaint.

The law would surely back him up.

There was a knock on the door.

'Who is it?' came back the surly reply from within.

'Only me, boss, Spike Dempster from down on the bar.'

'What d'yuh want at this hour?'

It was only ten in the morning. Not the time of day that Wade Garvey was at his best.

'There's a guy out here wants to speak with you,' he called rather diffidently. It didn't do to get on the wrong side of Wade Garvey. 'I told him you don't receive callers until after eleven, but he says it's urgent. Won't take no for an answer.'

A muffled curse echoed back from the other side of the door.

Suddenly it was thrown open. And there stood the sour-faced gang leader, legs apart, wiping bacon grease off his scowling visage with a white napkin.

'What's this crap all about?' he railed bluntly.

A little man stepped from behind the ponderous bulk of the bartender. He surveyed the room. Three other occupants were seated at a large table greedily shovelling food down their necks.

The visitor ignored them.

'My name is Aaron Spedding,' he said, in a pompous rather pushy tone. 'I'm the new barber in Buckeye, and I've come about this . . .' – he paused trying to inject a hint of mordancy into the delivery – 'this insurance agreement.'

'Have you signed it then?' The blunt question was delivered with venom.

'I don't do business with people who threaten me.' Unfazed, the barber continued his fit of umbrage by waving the paper in Garvey's face. 'And when I do

60

decide to take out some insurance, it will be conducted through a reputable company.'

Until that moment, the gang leader's features had been in shadow and hidden by the napkin. Now, he stepped forward, the waxed moustache twitching with unsuppressed anger.

'You callin' me a thief, mister?' Jabbing a finger into the barber's pudgy face, he didn't wait for an answer. 'I say who takes out insurance in this town. So you better drop that high 'n mighty tone and pay up. Savvy?'

'We'll see what the marshal has to say about that,' huffed Spedding. 'There's a law against racketeering in this state.'

Laughter erupted from the other occupants of the room.

'This turkey thinks that Hoot Cresswell's gonna arrest the boss,' hollered Mace Foggerty. The jasper's next derisive comment was aimed squarely at the barber. 'Who do you figure pays the marshal's salary, jughead?'

Garvey didn't join in with the hilarity. He was rapidly losing patience with this jumped-up tub of lard.

A rabid snarl issued from between puckered lips. Grabbing hold of the little man, he shook the quaking barber, making his eyes roll back in their sockets. Teeth bared in fury, Garvey thrust out his jutting chin. Aaron almost recoiled under the reeking onslaught of fatback and sour mash whiskey wafting over him.

But it was the gang leader's next iteration that stayed any adverse reaction.

'Hear that, mister? Me! Wade Garvey!'

He threw the barber aside like a sack of flour. The others laughed at the little man's discomfort.

'You tell him, boss,' spat Whip Kendrick, another of Garvey's hired hands. Aaron staggered and fell, cracking his head on a dresser. The sharp pain was ignored as round eyes bulged in shock.

*Wade Garvey!*

Could it really be one and the same?

And that wasn't all.

The light thrown on to the gang leader's contours by a smoky tallow lamp had outlined the impression of a ragged dent running from mouth to ear. The beard was gone, the black hair now streaked with a liberal dose of grey. But that wicked scar remained, just as he had remembered it after all these years.

Could his quest for retribution have arrived at last?

He would have to play this very carefully.

Quickly Aaron shrugged off his previous attitude of the outraged victim of fraud. Instead he adopted a far more compliant manner. Obsequiously fawning over the gang boss, he apologized profusely.

'I-I am very sorry for barging in here, Mr Garvey,' he bleated, rubbing his hands together. 'I don't know what came over me. Of course I agree to your terms.'

Garvey frowned. He was unsure of this sudden turnaround. Shrugging his shoulders, he assumed his browbeating had payed off. It sure saved him a heap of bother. Peering down his hawkish snout, he sniffed derisively, then handed the toadying barber a pen.

Aaron dutifully signed it.

'First payment due at the end of the week,' Garvey snapped, as he grabbed the form back and slotted it into a file that Aaron couldn't help noticing was full of similar such documents. 'Failure to pay on time could result in a visit from my, erm . . .' – Garvey chuckled as the right word was framed by his cruel lips – 'bailiffs. You've already met my chief negotiator, Mr Jack Patch. So you are aware of his methods.'

Aaron responded with a servile nod then turned to leave.

Patch accorded the shuffling excuse an insolent leer.

'Be seeing you soon, Mr Spedding,' he scoffed, throwing a gnawed beef rib, the sharp edge of which caught Aaron on his smooth pate.

'Good shot, Jack,' clucked Mace Foggerty.

Aaron uttered a sharp squawk of pain, but managed to hold himself in check. It was not easy.

He stumbled out of the office as the door slammed shut behind him. Cussing under his breath, he hawked a globule of spittle on to the carpet. His mind was in turmoil. Seething with indignation, he was nevertheless filled with exhilaration that his quest was reaching its zenith. Not only had he inadvertently found the killer of his father, in the very same room was the bastard who had defiled his sister. It was almost too much to absorb.

He needed a drink to calm his fraught nerves. A

chance to think straight and come to terms with this totally unexpected turn of events.

Not wishing to be observed by anyone in the bar, he left the saloon by the back stairs and scuttled back to the shop as fast as his chubby bow legs could move. The threatened storm had passed by to the south, leaving in its wake a blue sky streaked with horsetails of white to help lighten Aaron's mood.

Ten minutes later, he was ensconced with a bottle in his room above the shop. A satisfied smile played across the ruddy features as the hard liquor made its presence felt. All he needed to determine now was in what form his revenge could best be achieved.

That was going to be the difficult bit.

# SEVEN

# BATH TIME!

It was mid morning, five days after Aaron had first set eyes on Wade Garvey's new hireling.

The barber's shop was empty so he was taking a breather in the company of a strong mug of Arbuckles. The coffee jug was always kept brewing on the pot-bellied stove in the middle of the salon. It was another touch that his customers appreciated, the last of whom had only just left.

There was always a lull about this time. Aaron had maintained a sharp lookout for the hired gunfighter since his arrival in Buckeye. Each day the guy had left town heading in a different direction, clearly hoping to discover some clue as to the identity of the elusive killer of Wade Garvey's henchmen.

So far without success, a result that brought a tight smile to the barber's ruddy complexion. Initially, the little man had been exceedingly alarmed that this guy Nevado, the so-called top troubleshooter, might quickly expose the real culprit.

But after five days, with no indication of any accusing fingers being pointed in his direction, the barber had adopted a blasé attitude. Knowing that he was above suspicion imbued him with the confidence to put the guy to the test and really make him earn that hefty retainer. The only trouble was that Garvey had recently installed a washroom for his men behind the hotel. In consequence they had no need of Aaron Spedding's bathhouse facilities.

Maybe that was about to change.

Aaron's back straightened.

Strutting arrogantly across the street, was the perfect opportunity. Whip Kendrick was casually flicking his tell-tale rawhide snake at an unfortunate mutt that had inadvisedly chosen to snap at his heels. The deadly serpent split the air, cracking across the poor brute's back and evoking an agonized yelp. Even from behind the glass window of his salon, the barber could hear the rancid curse of the swaggering hardcase. The dog quickly backed off, disappearing beneath the wooden boardwalk to avoid further punishment.

Kendrick continued in a direct line.

Quite clearly he had a haircut in mind. And none too soon, mused the barber, sniffing imperiously at the dishevelled greasy thatch hanging limply beneath the Texas sombrero. As the mean-eyed tough shouldered through the door into the salon, Aaron was hard pressed not to reveal another desperately needed service. The abhorrent nose-twitching odour brought tears to his eyes, not to mention a soured twist to the fleshy mouth.

'Some'n wrong with you, barber?' growled the keen-eyed gunman.

'Just a bit of grit in the eye,' replied Aaron, assuming a blank expression as he dabbed a handkerchief at the offending orb. Struggling to control the quaver in his voice, he asked casually, 'I thought you boys had been given your own amenities?'

Kendrick uttered a derisive snort.

'That's OK for a general scrubdown, but I want the whole works,' he demanded, slumping into a chair. 'And don't skimp on that special lotion the boys have been talkin' about.'

'Does that mean you want a bath as well as a haircut, sir?' enquired the barber, trying hard to maintain a servile tone to his tightening vocal chords.

'Said I want the whole business, didn't I?'

The waspish retort was received with docile acquiescence.

'Certainly, sir.'

Aaron's thoughts were skipping ahead as he handed the gunman a mug of coffee and began stropping a cut-throat razor. His mouth set in a thin line as the glinting blade flashed back and forth.

But this was neither the time nor the place.

'Unfortunately, I've run out of hot water for the bathhouse.' Apologizing profusely, Aaron proceeded with the close shave. 'If sir would kindly return at five this afternoon, I will personally guarantee you the finest bathtime this side of the Mississippi . . .' – he paused for effect – 'and you will be completely undisturbed.'

Even though Aaron was filled with a nervous anticipation of what he was planning for this heap of pig manure, his hand remained rock steady. Tightly clutching the lethal razor, the barber's face remained expressionless, even though the flinty azure evident in the staring eyes was a dead giveaway. It was lucky that Kendrick had his peepers closed as Aaron carefully placed the razor to one side and deftly applied the shaving soap.

The hardcase grumbled some about the delay, but was easily persuaded, mollified by the barber's manner.

'In fact,' he gushed, turning on the oily charm that had become second nature. 'I have just taken delivery of a new hair restorative direct from Paris, France. And you will be the first to enjoy the benefit of its invigorating properties.'

This was his *pièce de resistance* owing to Kendrick's distinct shortage in that department.

'Sounds good,' preened the hardcase. 'That new gal we've taken on at the Texas Belle won't be able to resist old Whip smellin' like a bunch of roses.'

'Indeed she won't,' asserted the barber aiming a malevolent glare at the greying thatch. 'You'll have them all pining after you.'

The lethal razor hovered inches from the gunman's throat. Just a quick slash and it would all be over.

Shrugging off the notion, Aaron proceeded with

the job in hand as if he hadn't a care in the world. Once it was completed to Kendrick's satisfaction, Aaron bid him good day with the reminder not to let his buddies in on the new attraction.

'Why not?' shot back the gunsel, pausing in the doorway.

'You don't want any of the others stealing your glory, do you?' Aaron was more concerned that Kendrick's sidekicks should remain ignorant of their confederate's visit to the barber after hours. They might well jump to the right conclusions once the cat was out of the bag. And that would never do. 'Not to mention Lily May Carson,' added the little fellow with a knowing grin.

Kendrick considered the idea, then gave a sagacious nod.

'You're right, barber. Them turkeys ain't got no loyalty where women are concerned.'

'Our secret then?' pressed Aaron tapping his bulbous snout mindfully.

'Sure thing,' concurred the gunman returning the gesture.

The last customer had departed the salon a half-hour before Kendrick was due to arrive. Putting up the closed sign, Aaron now had plenty of time to prepare the bathhouse for his unsuspecting guest. The lone high-backed tub was turned so that it faced away from the door. A vital necessity for what the barber had in mind.

There was a knock on the outer door exactly as the

wall clock struck five. A cold smile flitted across the barber's round face. The ominous tolling sounded like a death knell. A fitting inception for what was about to follow.

He hurriedly opened the door and ushered his unsuspecting customer inside, quickly casting a wary eye along the street to ensure nobody was taking an unwelcome interest in this out-of-hour's transaction.

'This way, Mr Kendrick.' Aaron ushered the gunman into the back room indicating where he should place his grubby clothes. The cloying aroma emanating from the steaming bath tub couldn't disguise the fact that they ought to be burned. Suffice it to say, Aaron held his peace on that subject. 'Once you have bathed,' he added, 'I will give your head a full massage with the new lotion.'

Kendrick uttered an eager sigh of anticipation as the barber quietly left the room.

From the salon, Aaron could hear the bather humming a tuneless ditty totally ignorant of his imminent fate. Had he stopped, Whip Kendrick might have wondered why the barber was vigorously stropping a razor.

Satisfied that his victim was fully engaged with his ablutions, Aaron silently opened the bathhouse door. He had ensured that the hinges were well greased to avoid any warning squeaks. Stepping through into the steamy atmosphere, three quick strides and he was behind the splashing bather.

Anchored to the spot, eyes now burning red with

the heat of vengeance, his right arm lifted, the lethal razor hovering.

Then it happened.

Ever the consummate gunman, Kendrick must have sensed the presence lurking behind him.

'Who's there?' he hollered, turning his soapy head towards the sound of heavy breathing to his rear. At the same time, he lunged for the holstered revolver always close to hand.

But he was too late.

With a single fluid motion, Aaron struck. The razor's honed edge bit deep into the victim's neck. Blood spurted from the fatal wound, quickly staining the scummy water a bright red. It was all over in a flash. Aaron had perfected the technique over recent months. A final choked gurgle and the body slid beneath the greasy surface. Aaron held the jerking head down until no further movement could be felt.

Then he stood back. Grabbing at the wall for support, he sucked huge mouthfuls of air into his panting lungs. Slowly the tension eased from taut muscles, the dilated pupils of his eyes returning to their normal owlish regard.

Boy! Did he need a proper drink. Returning to the salon, he dropped into a chair and imbibed a hefty slug of whiskey. The fiery spirit eventually calmed his trembling frame. Only then could he begin to think straight.

The reaction after a killing was always the same. With the promise of revenge burning as fiercely in his heart, it never occurred to him that he was becoming immune to the taking of human life. Aaron Spedding recognized that he was never going to be a lady's man, but the mixture of fear and excitement made for a potent aphrodisiac.

He uttered a manic chuckle, demonic in its intensity. Wade Garvey and Jack Patch would be shaking in their boots tomorrow.

'Your turn will come soon enough,' murmured the little man toasting himself in the mirror. 'Cheers, Aaron!'

On further reflection, he knew that sooner or later his luck was bound to run out. Just so long as he nailed the two rats he was really after prior to that inevitable conclusion, then he could go to join the souls of his dearest departed with a clear conscience.

It was after midnight before all traces of the killing had been removed from the bathhouse. Wrapped in a blanket, the body of Whip Kendrick had been placed in a buggy out back ready for disposal.

That time had now arrived.

It was essential to wait until the town had settled down for the night before Aaron could safely leave by a back trail. As on previous occasions, he headed west, forking into the main trail after three miles. He knew exactly where to leave the body so that it would be quickly discovered on the morrow.

A crescent moon glowed silvery behind a scudding bank of light cloud bathing the rugged terrain with a diaphanous glow. The breathtaking pageant of sparkling diamonds that studded the night sky went unheeded.

Aaron reined in the trotting sorrel. A night owl hooted over to his left. After listening carefully for a full minute, he gave a satisfied nod before gigging the cayuse back into motion. Only the low sighing of the night breeze disturbed the all-encompassing silence.

Soon, however, the source of light faded, the moon smothered by a thick blanket transforming the landscape to an opaque grey.

Progress slowed to a walk. The last thing Aaron needed was to stray off the hard-packed dirt trail allowing the buggy to become stuck in the soft sandy borders. In consequence, it took longer than on the three previous occasions to reach his destination.

Eventually the bold outline of Cathedral Butte hoved into view. Etched starkly against the muted western horizon, the soaring landmark stood at a major crossroad: straight ahead to the Mexican border and El Paso, north across the Alvarez plateau into the territory of New Mexico.

Herds of longhorns moving up the Goodnight-Loving Trail passed this way frequently at this time of year. Kendrick's body would be easily spotted at the junction by some eagle-eyed cowpoke.

Because of the delay in reaching Cathedral Butte, it was almost dawn when the barber at last found himself entering the town limits of Buckeye. He was none too soon. Creeping remorselessly above the scalloped eastern rim of the Del Norte mountains, a pale orange backdrop streaked with pastel shades of pink and blue heralded the approach of the new day. Thankfully the town was still slumbering in the arms of Morpheus.

# EIGHT

# UNCHARTED WATERS

Nevado was having breakfast in the dining-room of the Imperial. The plate of eggs over easy and two slices of thick ham smothered in fried potatoes lay untouched. His mind was elsewhere. In fact he was trying to figure out what excuses he could give to his employer for not yet having delivered up the killer of his men.

This was proving to be a much tougher proposition than he had anticipated. On previous jobs, he had always known who he was after. It was just a matter of trailing the galoots, then calling the shots. Playing detective was much harder than he had imagined. And if something didn't come up soon, he was going to be in deep shit.

One to one, he could easily beat any of Garvey's men to the draw; only Jack Patch was likely to give him any trouble. But critters like them didn't play that sort of game. He would be a sitting duck for any hidden sniper.

No. He was going to have to pull a rabbit out of the hat. But the white-haired gunfighter knew that he was no music-hall magician.

'Food not to your liking then?'

The silky vocals caressed the back of his neck. Miss Penelope Wilson was every inch the classy dame who stopped men in their tracks and had their wives enviously eyeing her with daggers drawn. Lustrous red hair cascaded over slim shoulders like the Rio Grande in full spate; beneath, the elegant sculpting of a woman who knew her way around. She was wearing a closely fitting emerald-green dress which exhibited all her best features to perfection.

Even with such a vision of loveliness hovering at his elbow, the finest Parisian scent assaulting his olfactory organ, Nevado remained oblivious, unmoved.

The manageress of the Imperial bristled, an irksome frown besmirching the flawless complexion. She was unused to such an indifferent reaction to her presence. It was one reason why the hotel's dining-room was invariably filled with the more properous male members of the community.

Hands firmly planted on voluptuous hips and her heaving bosom directly in the firing line, Penny Wilson repeated the query, this time in a more spirited vein.

'You hear me?' she sang out. 'I asked you if there

was something wrong with the food.'

On this occasion. the curt demand jerked Nevado out of his lethargic torpor. The display of bare flesh up close was an equal shock to his system.

'Beg your pardon, ma'am,' he muttered, trying to shake out the cobwebs. 'Are you speaking to me?'

'You're darned right I am, fella.' She aimed a beringed digit at the untouched plate in front of the gunfighter. 'The food. Something wrong with it? Eggs too hard, potatoes not crispy enough?'

Nevado's face assumed a russet hue of embarrassment when he realized that all eyes in the room were locked on to this unwanted confrontation.

'My most humble apologies, Miss Penny,' he mumbled, quickly taking up his knife and fork and spearing a potato. 'Food's excellent, no complaints at all. Pass my compliments to the cook.' He paused, the potato hanging limply in mid air as the imminent meeting with Wade Garvey once again elbowed to the fore. 'Got things on my mind this morning, that's all.'

'You work for Garvey, don't you?' she asked, in a quieter voice. The question was superfluous as everybody knew the reason for the white-haired gun fighter being in Buckeye.

Nevado nodded.

Taking a seat, Penny Wilson poured them both a cup of coffee. This guy wasn't like the normal class of lowlife with which Wade Garvey surrounded himself. The gunfighter exuded an air of mystery that she found utterly intriguing.

'Seems to me like you ain't no hard-ass villain like Jack Patch or Mace Foggerty.' The statement was bluntly delivered, the follow-up acidly cutting. 'So what's a guy like you doing on the payroll of that scumbag?'

Nevado looked up from his meal, stunned by the harsh, brittle edge to the hotel-owner's query.

'I'm just here to find a killer. Once that's done, I'll be on my way.'

'Have gun, will travel. That's what they say of hired guns, isn't it?'

Nevado shrugged. 'It's a living.'

Penny Wilson's interest in the enigmatic drifter was more than just a passing fancy. During the short period of his stay, she had sensed a tormented soul imprisoned within that macho exterior, an agonized demon struggling to be exorcized. Perhaps she could help him to lay whatever nightmares were plaguing his life to rest.

Neither had it escaped her notice that Nevado was an exceedingly handsome figure of a man.

By the time the hired gunfighter had finished his breakfast, the dining-room had emptied. He pushed his plate aside with a sigh of satisfaction.

'Don't ever think that I don't appreciate either your vittles' – he peered deep into the woman's velvety eyes, drowning in their hypnotic allure – 'or your most welcome company. Perhaps you would do me the honour of riding out with me one day?'

It was now Penny's turn to blush, her eyelashes fluttered, the full lips pouting. Though she still maintained a somewhat reticent manner. When all was said and done, this guy was still working for a snake in the grass whom she held in utter contempt.

'I'll think about it,' she said with an eloquent air of hauteur, although she suspected what her answer would be if he asked her again.

At that moment, the front door of the hotel crashed open rattling the glass panels. Thoughts of an idyllic picnic by the river were thrust aside as loud voices broke into their dreamy reflections.

'We wanna see the boss.' The gravel-choked demand was instantly recognized by Nevado as that belonging to one of Garvey's confederates – a squint-eyed desperado by the name of Shifty Cornwell. He was one of the gang leader's more recent employees.

'Miss Wilson is otherwise engaged at the moment,' replied the hotel clerk in a seriously affected manner. 'If you would kindly leave your name and business, I will inform her that you called.'

A muted growl was followed by a scuffling and a high-pitched squeal that sounded like a newborn hog under the knife.

'You ain't listenin', chicken shit,' snapped the tough. 'I wanna see her *now*.' The last word was punched out with venom and accompanied by a heavy thud.

A choked cry issued from Penny's open mouth.

Nevado leapt to his feet. Palming and checking the load of his revolver, he made for the source of the fracas.

Penny quickly laid a restraining hand on his arm.

'Let me deal with this,' she said tersely. Any notions of a possible liaison between the two was fast dissolving as the reality of their differing positions in the town elbowed to the fore. 'If I'm not mistaken, it's your boss's jackals come for the insurance premium. And you wouldn't want to bite the hand that feeds you, eh?' The acerbic inflection was not lost on the hired gunfighter. And it hurt. 'I can handle varmints like them,' she added.

Without a backward glance, Penny strode purposefully into the opulent foyer where her ashen-faced clerk was picking himself up off the floor. A red smear dribbled from a cut lip.

'There was no need for that sort of treatment,' she asserted vehemently, instantly perceiving that the glowering Shifty Cornwell was accompanied by Chocktaw Pete. 'You'll get your money.' She turned to address the distraught clerk. 'Are you all right, Ambrose?'

The tottering man dabbed at his injured mouth, replying with a brief nod as he fearfully eyed the swaggering bully boys.

'Go into the parlour and have Maisie see to that cut,' she ordered, ushering the frightened man out of harm's way. 'I'll deal with these . . . gentlemen.'

'Are you sure, Miss Penny?' the little man asked, trying desperately to recover his composure.

'Yes, yes. Now off you go,' she clucked.

Turning back to the visitors, she spat out. 'You're two days early. Garvey doesn't normally let his dogs out of their kennel until Saturday. Tell him that I'll pay him then and not before.'

Visibly stung by the caustic insult, Cornwell uttered a rancid curse. His left eye twitched fractiously. Lunging forward, he grabbed the woman by the hair violently wrenching her neck back. She emitted a tortured scream.

'Nobody speaks to me like that,' Cornwall rapped. A bunched fist was raised, intent on delivering a stunning blow that would easily have laid her out cold.

It never landed.

A grip of iron held the swinging appendage prisoner. Nevado had no intention of allowing Miss Penelope Wilson to be manhandled by any man, let alone some lowlife skunk from the Texas Belle. And when the bastard had resorted to physical retaliation for a slight he had more than deserved, the gunfighter had made it his business to even out the odds somewhat.

'What the hell. . . ?'

Shifty Cornwell had not been aware of the gunfighter's presence and was taken by surprise.

Twisting the roughneck's arm behind his back, Nevado flung him headlong at the wall. Cornwell bounced off the solid barrier hitting the equally hard floor with a bone-jarring crunch. But the hardcase was no mollycoddle and was soon back on his feet.

When he saw who it was had upended him, a look of stunned amazement halted the desperado's blundering rush to hit back.

'You!' he exclaimed. 'So the hired gun has changed into a treacherous snake. The boss ain't gonna be pleased when he hears that you've been interferin' in his business affairs. I figure he'd expect more loyalty, especially with what you're bein' paid – a heap more'n the rest of us.'

'You tell him that I don't like the way his rat-faced underlings carry out their duties,' retorted Nevado, his hand hovering above the butt of his pistol just in case the rabid critter was rash enough to call him out.

That was the moment when Penny Wilson's sharp vocals cut through the tense atmosphere. Both men turned to face her.

'Hold it right there, fella!'

A cocked double-barrelled Loomis shotgun was pointed at the stomach of Chocktaw Pete. The 'breed had sidled up behind Nevado and was about to lay him flat with a gun barrel.

'Just step back apace, Pete.' snapped Penny, holding the Indian with a witheringly uncompromising glare. 'I'd hate for your miserable hide to stain my new wallpaper.'

The Indian was no talker, but he sure understood the meaning of a pointed gun, and that the woman holding it meant every damn word. He took a step back holstering his pistol, the expression on his wrinkled face blank and impenetrable.

'Now I think it's about time you gentlemen left,' enunciated the indignant hotel owner. Her words were delivered with a cogent bite. 'And keep them hands well clear of the hardware.'

Penny gestured towards the door with the shotgun.

Both of the intruders reluctantly backed out of the hotel.

Cornwell slung a finger in Nevado's direction.

'You ain't heard the last of this, mister,' he hissed. 'Not by a long shot. Mr Garvey's gonna be none too pleased that a hired hand has stopped his collection agents from goin' about their legitimate business.'

'Legitimate, my ass!' spat the hotel proprietor. 'Garvey's nothing but a jumped-up racketeer.'

Cornwell shot her a malevolent scowl, then slammed the door.

Nevado carefully removed the shotgun from Penny's trembling grasp and ushered her to a seat.

'A drink for Miss Wilson,' he called out to the skulking reception clerk. 'And make it a double.' Then, addressing the hotel proprietor he said, 'You sure ain't no shrinking violet, that's for sure.'

The glass of French brandy brought back the colour to her wan features. Although it was a full five minutes before Penny felt able to speak.

'Men figure they have all the angles covered.' Her barbed remark was laced with a lofty pride. 'Well, let me tell you, mister, that this little gal can stand on her own two feet.'

Then her large eyes softened as she realized that Nevado's presence in the hotel had prevented a noxious incident in which she could have been seriously injured.

Peering at her benefactor from beneath lowered eyebrows, she tentatively admonished him. 'Going up against Garvey like that is not likely to be good for your health,' she murmured. 'That critter is one mean son of Satan when things don't go his way. Maybe I should go down there right now and pay up. Tell him it was all a misunderstanding.'

She made to rise, but the gunfighter laid a hand on her arm.

'While I'm in Buckeye doing the job he hired me for, nothing is going to happen to me. And I'll make darned certain that from here on they treat you with respect.'

Penny shrugged his hand off, a fiery gleam in her eye.

'So you still intend remaining on Garvey's payroll?'

Nevado spread his hands as if the question of resigning hadn't entered his head.

'It appears then that you and I are still on different sides.' Her tone was frosty and dismissive. 'Perhaps you had better go and apologize to your boss and get on with this job he's paying you for. Then you can leave town with a clear conscience, and a full pocket.'

She stood up, smoothing down the rumpled dress and brushing a stray lock of hair from her blanched face.

'You are welcome to stay on at the Imperial as a paying guest,' she stated impassively, 'but I feel it more appropriate if our relationship is kept on a professional basis in future.'

Then she turned away, head held high, and left without a backward glance.

Nevado felt empty, deflated. The cutting invective had stung him like a slap in the face. Never before had he allowed his feelings to get in the way of the job for which he had been engaged. She was one feisty dame. And this woman had somehow pene- trated the tough shell of his very being. It was an experience that was both exhilarating yet at the same time confusing, and not a little alarming.

His mind was in a turmoil.

Could it be that his life as a hired gun was begin- ning to pall? Buzzing around inside his head, the notion was unsettling, a disturbing jolt to the life he had thrived on for so long: the excitement, the kudos of being the guy folks sought out to solve their prob- lems.

Then again there was the downside: being constantly on the move; one step ahead of any hard- nosed critter itching to take out the legendary Nevado; living on the edge, never quite knowing if the next bullet has your name on it; lonely hotel rooms with the only female company being that of soiled doves handing out false flattery to paying customers, their job merely to service the most basic need of their clients.

Sure the life paid well. And there was a sizeable balance in his bank account in Amarillo. Enough to buy a decent business once this current job was completed. But for that to be a worthwhile proposi- tion he needed a partner – a wife! Penny Wilson would have been the perfect choice.

But she had made it plain as day that a hired

gunfighter was not her idea of an eligible husband. And who could blame her.

Nevado left the Imperial with much to think on.

Crossing the busy street, the hustle around him went unnoticed. It was only when a galloping rider almost ran him down that his thoughts returned to the here and now.

'Watch where yer goin', fella! Crossin' a street like that'll buy yuh an early grave fer sure.'

The cowpuncher's vociferous outcry brought a raised hand of acknowledgement from the startled gunfighter. He quickly hurried over to the opposite boardwalk shaking loose the disrupting images that his recent experience at the Imperial had unleashed.

After all, he was still a professional.

And the idea of abandoning a job once agreed upon, was anathema to all he held true. Garvey might well be a low-life skunk, but he had accepted the dude's money and felt morally obligated to see it through. A strange code of honour to some perhaps, but one that had earned Nevado a degree of respect and esteem he was loath to cast aside.

Maybe in future, he would see things differently.

But for the present. . . .

# NINE

# A SCENTED RAT

Nevado extracted the sack of Bull Durham from his shirt pocket and deftly rolled a fresh quirly. Lighting up, he inhaled deeply allowing the blue smoke to trickle from between pursed lips. It was not until the stogie was burning his fingers that he felt ready to call on the devil in his own kitchen.

Garvey had been expecting his visitor. Indeed, if Nevado had not made an appearance when he had, the gang boss was all set to unleash his pack of wolves to hunt him down.

A grim expression did not augur well for the convocation.

'What's this I bin hearin' about you stickin' yer butt in where it ain't wanted?' Garvey's snarling demand brought a grunt of accord from the two bruisers on his right. Shifty Cornwell and the half-breed had obviously primed their boss well. 'You're bein' paid to hunt down a killer, not to interfere in my business dealings. And so far I ain't seen any results from my investment.'

Garvey thrust his square chin forward. challenging the gunfighter with a steely regard.

Nevado met his gaze unflinchingly, but remained tight-lipped.

'Well?' snapped Garvey. His ugly mouth curled in a sardonic leer. 'I need some answers.'

The affront was met with harsh guffaws from the two henchmen.

'You heard the boss, Mr Snow White,' sneered Jack Patch. 'When you gonna earn your dough?'

Even though he was surrounded by a half-dozen heavily armed gunmen, Nevado was all set to ram Patch's fractious comment down his throat, and to hell with the consequences. His reputation was at stake. Back down and he would be a laughing stock among this bunch of slimeballs.

Nerves strung tight as a drum head, he sucked in a deep breath.

It was Hoot Cresswell who saved the day.

Bursting in through the closed door, the marshal blurted out the grisly tidings that Garvey was loath to hear.

'Whip Kendrick's body has been found at the crossroads near Cathedral Butte.' He paused for breath having run all the way from the jailhouse down the street. The lawdog's bloated face was as red as the setting sun. 'His throat has been cut from ear to ear. Not a pretty sight according to Clint Weaver, the cowpoke who brought me the news.'

On hearing this disastrous revelation, Garvey's lower jaw hit the floor with a bang. He was stunned into silence, and scared shitless, although he made certain not to show it. Only a thin film of sweat on his forehead, quickly wiped away, betrayed the gang boss's trepidation. He was acutely aware that his own appointment with the grim reaper could only be a matter of time at this rate.

It was Nevado who broke the tense silence.

'Where's the body now?' he asked bluntly.

'Weaver left it there,' replied the marshal. 'He reckoned we would want to hear about it as quickly as possible.'

'Have you got a flatbed?' This to Garvey who responded with a stupefied nod. 'I'll go out there straight away and pick up the body. Scout around while I'm out there. Like as not the killer will have left some clue.'

Then he turned back to Cresswell. 'Did this rannie move the body at all?'

The marshal shook his head. 'Seein' that throat wound scared him off.'

Nevado had rapidly taken command of the situation. This could be just the break he had been hoping for. And he intended taking full advantage of the situation.

Still in a fog, Garvey was more than eager to oblige. He slumped into his seat. His previously arrogant bluster had dissolved like a snowball in hell. The hired gunfighter was now his only hope of coming through this critical situation unscathed.

His henchmen were equally deflated. More so than their boss, if the paled expressions of fear told the truth. It was their ranks that were being so systematically thinned.

'Show Mr Nevado where the wagon is kept, Mace.'

Foggerty haltingly gestured for him to follow.

Before leaving the sombre gathering, the hired gunfighter vibrantly assured them that this was the lead for which he had been waiting.

'Shame it had to be another stiff that pointed the way forward.' He shrugged, trying to conceal his euphoria. 'At least Whip Kendrick is going to be of more help in death than he ever was alive.'

A thin smile broke across the tanned features as hawkish eyes panned the fearful looks praying that he was right.

Before exiting from the office, he took a quick step towards Patch and slammed a bunched fist into the guy's midriff. It was followed by a stiff upper cut that tumbled the hardcase on to his back. Blood spurted from a split lip as Patch rolled over.

'Next time you address me, watch your mouth,' snapped Nevado blowing on his bruised knuckles.

Then he turned to leave.

But Jack Patch was no easy pushover and recovered quickly. Dragging a revolver from its holster, he thumbed the hammer to full cock and aimed it at the hired gun's retreating back. Garvey had seen the move and anticipated his lieutenant's instinctive reaction.

Quick as lightning, he moved round the desk. For

a man of his bulk, he was no sluggard. His right boot connected with Patch's gun hand sending the weapon spinning harmlessly into a corner.

'I'm the one giving the orders around here,' he snarled in the gunman's face. 'You deserved that, Jack. Now get yer ass downstairs and cool off.'

Nevada's rugged features cracked into a leering grin. He slammed the door closed and followed after Mace Foggerty.

But Patch was not finished with Nevado yet. The hardcase hustled to the door leading out the back of the saloon.

Nevado was below, climbing on to the wagon.

'This ain't the end of the matter, Snowy,' Patch growled, wiping a smear of blood from his mouth. 'When this business is straightened out, you and me can settle up as well.'

Nevado arrowed a disdainful grimace towards the bodyguard. 'I'll be waiting,' he smirked. 'Just be sure to bring some back-up. You'll need it.'

Patch spat out a list of garbled imprecations before retiring to the bar of the Texas Belle.

'You've made a bad enemy there, fella,' warned Mace Foggerty. 'Jack don't forget an insult.'

'Turkeys like that don't scare me none,' Nevado replied crisply. 'Now which way do I head for Cathedral Butte?'

Foggerty shrugged. It was none of his business.

Having been given directions by the subdued outlaw, Nevado took the trail out of Buckeye heading due west. The sun was high in the sky, sporadic hunches of white cumulus playing chase across the azure firmament.

Apart from the brief jolt given to his nervous system by Penny Wilson that morning, he was feeling all fired up and confident. This was surely going to be his best opportunity of solving the case, collecting the rest of his fee, and quitting Buckeye for good.

The town was soon left behind.

Rolling tracts of blue grama intermingled with clusters of buffalo grass. Soft zephyrs coaxed a gentle sway giving the impression of a land-locked ocean. Few trees broke the flatness of the plateaulands except along the disconnected arroyos.

A flight of quail arrowing past in a tight V formation educed an envious sigh from the gunfighter. Nevado couldn't help wondering if man could ever hope to emulate their dexterity. He scoffed at the notion. If humans had been meant to fly, the good Lord would have given them wings. As if to endorse this view, a pair of jack-rabbits scooted across the trail followed soon after by a skunk ambling at a far more leisurely pace.

'Keep your distance, fella,' warned Nevado, jigging the horse to a steady canter.

Apart from the occasional yucca and Joshua Tree, nothing disturbed the regular tabletop of the landscape. As far as the eye could see, the only break in the skyline came from the surging splinter of rock that was Cathedral Butte. The landmark could be seen for a full hour before the wagon finally arrived at the crossroads lying in its shadow.

Whip Kendrick's body was in full view, the ugly slash around the throat like a black collar, a stark reminder to Nevado of the deadly task he had undertaken. He immediately jumped to the conclusion that this must be a deliberate ploy so that the body would be quickly discovered. Whoever was behind the killings was eager to strike terror into Garvey and his men.

He was succeeding.

The entire front of the outlaw's shirt was caked in dried blood. It was little wonder that Clint Weaver had kept his distance. Bending over the stiffening corpse, Nevado's nose wrinkled at the smell. Not the odour of death of which he was eminently familiar; this was something different.

Nevado's face creased in thought. Tentatively, he bent down further and sniffed at the man's face. A sickly cloying aroma tickled his nasal passageway inducing a spasm of coughing. Another brief whiff and he stood up. Backing away, he imbibed the untainted plains air gratefully.

Stroking his stubbly chin, brow ribbed in a deep frown, the gunfighter knew that this smell had to be the key, the pivotal crux of his investigation.

He knew that odour. But what was its source?

Where would a hard-nosed critter like Whip Kendrick have acquired such a scent? It was more like something out of a whore's boudoir.

Stamping around the gruesome site, Nevado racked his brains. The answer had to be staring him in the face.

Then it struck him like a rampant tornado. Kendrick's hair was short, his smooth face having only recently been shaved. He must have visited the town barber late yesterday. So the smell could easily have resulted from bath lotion.

Could this be the answer?

It had been Nevado's intention to call upon the barber this very day for a similar service. The notion that he could have been the crimper's next victim propelled an icy shiver down his backbone. And he wouldn't have had an inkling of what was coming.

He sat down on the tailboard of the wagon pulling hard on a stogie to calm his nerve ends. He had faced death on many occasions. But this was the first time that the scythe man had almost crept up on him unannounced. The mortifying image portrayed was nightmarish in its intensity.

There was only one way to discover the truth, the conclusion as to whether or not Aaron Spedding was indeed the demon barber of Buckeye.

Nevado ran a hand through his unruly white locks. He would have to make that call. But on this occasion he would be prepared, ready with his own response to the cut-throat razor.

# TEN

# SUSPICIONS CONFIRMED

Once he had delivered the body of Whip Kendrick to the undertaker, Nevado headed for a saloon frequented by the cowmen. Following his discovery, the hired gunfighter was desperately in need of a drink. The Longhorn was far enough removed at the end of Main Street to avoid any unwelcome meeting with Jack Patch and his sidekicks. At this stage, he had no wish to share his suspicions with Wade Garvey or anyone else until he was sure that the little barber was indeed the culprit.

On the ride back to town, one question had been bugging him.

*Why would an inoffensive dude like Aaron Spedding be engaged in such a desperate manoeuvre?*

Only the little man himself could provide the answer to that conundrum.

Nevado shouldered through the batwings and sidled up to the bar. It was early afternoon and the saloon was almost empty. A couple of business types sat at a table discussing the price of beef. Three drovers lounged against the mahogany bar top sipping at foaming tankards of beer. Over in a corner, the house gambler was playing patience all on his ownsome.

Catching Nevado's eye, he indicated for the gunfighter to join him. Nevado's brisk response was a curt shake of the head. He was in no mood for concentrating on the finer points of black jack.

'A bottle of Kentucky bourbon if you've got it,' he asked the bartender, slamming a five-dollar piece on the counter.

'Sure do,' replied the rotund 'keep breezily, whilst reaching up to the top shelf behind him. 'You're lucky, mister. That's my last bottle. Don't get much call for it in these parts.' Pushing the dusty bottle across the shiny counter, he added, 'You from back East then?'

'And some.'

Idle chatter with a nosy barman was the last thing on his mind. The brief retort was sufficient to propel the guy to the other end of the bar where he resumed the ever-present task of glass polishing.

A half-hour later, with the bottle's contents fast diminishing, Nevado had worked out exactly how he would play this bizarre hand he had been dealt.

Clutching hold of the bottle, he turned to leave.

It was a comment from one of the cowhands that

made him pause in mid-stride.

'That must have been one helluva scary experi-ence, Clint,' proffered a tall rannigan sipping on his glass of beer. 'You comin' across that gunslick of Garvey's on the trail near Cathedral Butte.'

Clint Weaver replied with a sombre nod.

'Sure was, Brad. Shook me up some'n awful, I can tell yuh.' Weaver took a long slurp from his own pot before continuing, 'That's the second one I've come across. Both with their throats slit, and dumped in the very same spot.'

'Maybe you oughta take a different trail into town next time,' suggested the third cowboy.

'Or maybe he shouldn't be so eager to be first up of a mornin',' laughed the man called Brad.

The others joined in, but it was a stilted response lacking any humour. That was the moment Nevado chose to butt in.

'You Clint Weaver?' he enquired. 'The guy who found Whip Kendrick's body?'

All three cowboys turned to face the speaker.

'That's me,' replied the cowpoke affording Nevado a quizzical regard. 'Ain't you the fella brought in by Wade Garvey to clear this mess up?'

Nevado side-tracked the query with one of his own.

'Did the first guy you saw – Lex Mooney wasn't it?' – Weaver affirmed the notion with a brief nod – 'did he look the same as Kendrick?'

Weaver's response was a perplexed grimace.

'What yuh gettin' at, mister?'

Nevado had to choose his words carefully. He had no desire to reveal his suspicions yet awhile. And certainly not to these three jiggers.

'Well,' he began, 'did they both have a similar appearance, not counting their clothes, of course?'

The young cowpoke gave the query some thought, then said, 'They both had short hair, if that's what you mean. And were clean-shaven.' Weaver's eyes widened as an idea came to him. 'Come to think of it, they both looked as if they'd recently paid a visit to the barber.' Having voiced his opinion, the cowboy's shoulders lifted in a shrug. 'Apart from that. . . .'

Nevado's face remained impassive, empty of feeling. This was just what he had wanted to hear, but he kept that knowledge safely locked away behind the deadpan expression.

'Never mind,' he sighed, as if the disclosure was of little help to him. 'Sorry to have troubled you.' Extracting a five-dollar piece, he slammed it on the bar announcing, 'Have a drink on me, boys.'

With free drinks on offer, any thoughts regarding the gunfighter's inquisitive probing instantly disappeared.

'Much obliged,' grinned an open-mouthed Clint Weaver who, along with his buddies, had been nursing a small beer for the last hour with no chance of another until payday.

Returning to the hotel, Nevado was intercepted by Jack Patch.

'You brought in Kendrick's body?' glowered the man in black, caressing the bone handle of his revolver with menacing intent. He still reckoned that one to one, he could easily take on the hired gun in a duel, and win. Patch had convinced himself that on the trail, he had been unprepared, caught unawares. Next time, he would be ready.

'Dropped it off at the undertaker's,' replied the hired gun.

'The boss wants to know if you've figured out who the killer is yet.'

'You tell him that I'm on the case. Just got a few ends to tie up. He can expect a result before long.'

'And when's that gonna be?' pressed the gunman with an arrogant sneer.

Nevado extracted a cheroot from his vest and lit up, all the while holding the other man's pernicious gaze. This guy was beginning to get under his skin. Heavy brows knitted over hooded eyes as the curt reply was delivered with measured calculation. 'When I'm good and ready.'

Nevado made to push past the burly hardcase.

But Patch stood his ground. Maybe now was the time to call this high-and-mighty bastard.

'That ain't good enough,' he snarled, flexing his gunhand. Patch vividly recalled the last occasion they had met and Nevado's brusque reaction to his taunting remarks. The bloody evidence was still clearly visible on the bodyguard's cheek.

The pair of gunslingers faced each other no more than six feet apart. Both were ready, hunkered down into the classic stance. Set rigid like statues waiting for the moment when one of them would go for his gun.

That moment never arrived. It was a call from across the street that broke the deathly tension.

'Hey, Jack!'

It was Ace Montana.

'Yeh?' Patch's irritable reply was curtly delivered.

'Boss wants to see you.'

'Tell him I'll be there in a minute,' he rasped.

'He said right away,' urged Montana sensing that he had intervened in something personal. Knowing his sidekick's brash nature, the gambler laid stress on the gang boss's order. 'You don't wanna keep him waitin' now, do you Jack?'

Patch hesitated, but the moment for a showdown had passed. His body relaxed as he stepped back apace. A mirthless grin cracked the hard exterior of the weathered planes of his face.

'Seems like Lady Luck has stepped in to save your miserable hide,' he jeered, aiming a gloved finger at Nevado. 'But there'll be another time. You and me ain't finished yet, mister.'

Nevado slung a thumb towards the Texas Belle. 'Better not keep the boss waiting, Jack,' he smirked. 'He might not like it.' Then, with a insolent guffaw, he elbowed the gunman aside and sauntered off down the street.

On entering the foyer of the Imperial, he almost collided with Penny Wilson who was on her way out.

'My apologies, Miss Wilson,' he bowed, stepping to one side.

The proprietor blushed. It was an awkward moment. This was the first time they had met since

Penny had effectively terminated any thoughts of a more intimate liaison the hired gunfighter might have entertained. Each had purposefully kept out of the other's way.

'N-no harm done,' she stuttered, trying not to catch his eye.

'And how are you keeping?' enquired Nevado, himself somewhat taken aback.

'Very well, thank you.'

The silence that followed was strained, uncomfortable.

'Perhaps we could have a drink together sometime?' suggested Nevado tentatively. 'Talk things over.'

Penny brushed the notion aside.

'I don't think so, Mr Nevado.' The response was briefly curt. 'There is nothing more to be said on the matter.' Gathering up her fallen purse, she hustled out of the hotel without another word.

Nevado was crestfallen. He had figured that time might have healed the rift between them. His assumption was clearly wrong.

Across the street, a malicious grin broke across Jack Patch's face. He fingered the tender abrasion on his cheek. Nevado's brush-off by the girl was worth all the ribbing he had suffered at the hands of the other gang members.

Back in his hotel room, Nevado lay on his bed. Smoke from the black cheroot drifted on the fetid air as he tried to dispel thoughts of Penny Wilson from his turbulent brain. Each time he attempted to focus on how he was going to tackle the problem of Aaron Spedding, the girl's lustrous image kept intruding.

Eventually he fell asleep.

# ELEVEN

# THE TRAP IS SPRUNG

It was early evening when he awoke. Opening his pocket watch, the dial read 5.38. The hauntingly beautiful tune that chimed forth reinforced the vengeful task he had set himself all those years ago, just as it always did. A single teardrop etched a trail down his lined face. Until he had finally purged himself, there could be no place in his life, or indeed his heart, for a vision of loveliness such as Penny Wilson.

With that resolution settled, he swung his long legs off the bed and splashed cold water into a basin. Stripping down to his pants, a liberal dousing sought to dispel the feeling of lethargy that had been niggling at his innards. Donning a freshly laundered shirt, he felt ready to confront a killer.

From his window in the Imperial, Nevado had an uninterrupted view along Main Street down to the barber's shop. Following the departure of the last customer, it was Spedding's normal routine to sweep out the discarded hair on to the boardwalk.

On perceiving the barber thus engaged, Nevado strapped on his gunbelt and hustled down the back stairs of the hotel. Quickly scuttling along a back alley, he emerged on to the main street three blocks west, adjacent to the barber's shop.

'Any chance of a bath before you close up?' he enquired, with nonchalant ease, adding, 'Sorry I've left it to the last minute, but Garvey wanted to know how I was getting on with my investigations.'

Spedding laid aside his broom.

'Any luck finding the killer?' The barber's casual enquiry belied a nervous inflection that he concealed with a brisk cough.

At the same time he was thinking that here was a heaven-sent opportunity to dispose of another of that skunk's henchmen. And not any ordinary hired hand. Here was being presented the chance of getting rid of the principal adversary, the one man capable of sniffing out his deathly scheme of vengeance.

'This job has got me beat.' Nevado removed his hat, scratching his head in affected bewilderment. 'If truth be told,' he whispered conspiratorially, 'I'm thinking of leaving town. Pulling out while my throat's still intact.'

Spedding could barely contain his elation.

He ushered the white-haired gunfighter into the salon.

'Just sit down here while I fill up a bath,' he purred, a benign smile crimping his pudgy features.

'Any of that fancy lotion available?' asked Nevado.

'A fresh batch arrived only yesterday,' gushed the hovering barber. 'All the way from Paris, France.' He could hardly wait to sharpen up his razor.

Fifteen minutes later, the barber called his intended victim through into the bath house. Nevado felt like a fly being lured into the spider's web. Even though he held all the aces, it was nevertheless a disconcerting situation. Entering the hot steamy den, he couldn't help but shiver, knowing what the barber had on his evil mind.

So this was where it had all taken place.

The execution chamber! And there in front – his very own killing field.

The tin bath was facing away from the salon door as expected. And from it arose that clinging aroma, the very essence of death. Nevado struggled to contain the bile rising from his stomach. To spill his guts on to the damp floor now would surely give the game away.

'Just hang your clothes on a peg and give me a shout when you are finished,' warbled the barber, oblivious to his customer's chagrin. Then he added with thoughtful intent, 'Better leave your firearm with me. It'll rust up in this damp atmosphere.'

A bit of insurance in case of some mishap to his nefarious plan, mused Nevado. This guy had all the angles covered. He uttered a silent prayer that he had seen fit to retain a tiny derringer in his boot.

Once Spedding had retired to the outer salon, the hired gunfighter made his own plans. Removing his hat, he carefully placed it on the back rim of the bath tub to appear as if the wearer was still ensconced in the hot water.

Stepping out of the barber's line of sight when he entered the room, he waited whilst warbling a popular melody as all bathers are prone to do on such occasions.

Time appeared to hang suspended in the hot air.

In reality, it was less than two minutes before the door slowly swung open on the well-greased hinges. Creeping noiselessly into the room, the barber's attention was completely focused on the hat and its supposed owner. The odious gleam in his beady eyes was repellant to behold.

The cut-throat rose anticipating a soft neck to slice open.

That was when Nevado made his move. Stepping forward in a single fluid movement, he smashed the tiny gun down on to the barber's outstretched arm, knocking the razor from his grasp. It plopped uselessly into the soapy water.

Spedding yelped. The shock of having the tables suddenly upended stunned him into immobility. He was no grappler, having always relied on his wits to wriggle out of trouble. And the gun jammed into his ear brooked no argument.

Then his quaking voice returned.

'Don't shoot, mister,' he begged. 'Please. It ain't how it seems.'

'Don't give me that hogwash,' shot back Nevado, an arm firmly slung round the guy's stubby neck while the derringer prodded his twitching snout. 'You been caught all set to slit my gizzard, just like you done those other poor saps who walked in here figuring they were going to enjoy a nice bath. Don't try and wriggle out of it cos you've been rumbled.'

Spedding's corpulent frame sagged as the full realization that the game was finally up sank in. His eyes dulled, the ruddy complexion paling as blood drained from the puffy cheeks. Nevado hustled him over to a chair which he slumped into like a sack of potatoes.

Head bowed in total dejection, he asked, 'How did you cotton on?'

Nevado gave the question a terse laugh.

'You shouldn't have made such an issue of that special lotion. It's strong stuff. And the whiff lingers. Kendrick still reeked of it when I found him the next day. And there was only one place he could have acquired a pretty-boy smell like that, wasn't there?'

Sad doleful eyes peered back at him.

'I suppose you are going to drag me over to face Garvey now,' he intoned morosely. A pleading look creased Spedding's haggard profile. 'Do me a favour, mister, and get it over with right here and now. Just pull that trigger and it'll be all over. You'll get your fee and can leave Buckeye having done a good job. Least you can do is put me out of my misery. It don't matter now that I've failed to get even with that bastard.'

Nevado speared him with a pensive frown. The tiny pocket gun remained rock steady, the trigger finger tight. This dude appeared on the surface to have had the stuffing knocked out of him. But he had still been instrumental in the brutal slaying of four tough *hombres* and Nevado had been lined up as the fifth to receive the barber's unique service.

'You talking about Garvey?' he asked curtly.

The query received a sorry nod of accord.

'So what has he done that's got you so all fired up?' This was the question that had dogged his thoughts ever since he had homed in on the culprit. 'It must have been something mighty serious.'

That's when it all poured out. This was the first time Aaron Spedding had relived his nightmare to another human being since that ghastly day all those years ago. Once the diatribe had been unleashed, it was obvious to Nevado that the guy was not lying. Nobody could put on a show like that.

Once he had finished, the little man appeared to regain some of his previous *joie de vivre*. It was as if the reliving of his nightmare had finally purged his soul.

'So that's it,' he said briskly. 'Now do your worst, Mister Hired Gunfighter. I don't care, one way or the other.'

The relating of the barber's frightful story had resurrected similar events from Nevado's past. His mind was in a quandary. This needed reflecting on.

Both men sat opposite each other. Only the gentle

hissing of the water boiler impinged on their ruminations.

It was Nevado who broke the taut silence.

He rose, set his hat straight, and made to leave the
bathhouse.

'I need time to figure this out,' he said. His words
emerged in a measured, even tone. 'You sure seem to
have just cause for what you've done. But that don't
mean I'm letting you off the hook. I'll come back
tomorrow morning and tell you what I've decided.'
He pointed a threatening finger towards the cowed
figure. 'And in the meantime, don't think of skipping town, cos if'n you do, I'll hunt you down and
personally carve your name on a Boot Hill coffin.'

'Don't worry,' replied the barber. 'Right now,
there ain't no place else I want to be.'

Nevado spent a restless night. His own traumatic
memories kept elbowing into the frame. On more
than one occasion, he woke up bathed in sweat and
gasping for breath. In the end, he just lay there awaiting the dawn, knowing it held few answers.

He was knocking on the barber's door as the opac-
ity of night was gradually being nudged aside.
Striations of pink and mauve spiked the eastern horizon heralding the arrival of the new day. Dark shadows melted away with the ascension of the burgeon-
ing sunrise when the little man answered the door.

Spedding was already dressed and awaiting his
caller. Unlike Nevado, he had passed a dreamless
and undisturbed night. Whatever its outcome, the

future now held no fears for him. He was fully prepared for the worst.

The hired gunfighter's opening gambit, however, was received with wide-eyed astonishment. Nevado came straight to the point.

'I'm pulling out this morning,' he announced without preamble. His horse was packed and ready for the trail. 'Your secret is safe with me. How you plan it from here on ain't no concern of mine. Far as I'm concerned, Garvey and his hirelings deserve all they get. So from here on, the ball's in your court.'

Spedding was anchored to the spot. Stunned into silence, his fleshy mouth flapped wildly. This was a totally unexpected turn of events.

Finally locating his voice, he asked, 'What are you going to tell Garvey?'

Nevado shrugged. 'Just that this job has got me beat. I'll return his fee and then light out.'

Spedding grabbed the gunfighter's hand and shook it.

'Much obliged,' he averred gratefully. 'I reckon it's about time for me to quit Buckeye as well.'

'Where you figure on heading?' asked Nevado.

'The county seat at Fort Stockton,' he said without hesitation. 'I'm going to give myself up to the sheriff and trust that Texas law will offer me some form of justice.'

'Well, good luck to you,' replied Nevado, turning on his heel.

'You can't leave now!'

It was later that morning. Wade Garvey was livid. But he was also scared. A hunted look flitted across the weathered features. Here was his only hope of finding the killer wanting to up sticks.

'I paid you good money up front to hunt down this killer,' railed the gang boss. 'Me and my boys need protection.' Puffing out his broad chest, Garvey went on, 'And what's this you've been telling Patch about almost solving the case?'

Nevado scowled. 'Well, I was wrong.' Then he threw a bulging envelope on to the desk. 'There's all your blood money returned, less expenses,' he countered firmly. 'You'll have to find somebody else.'

'Where am I gonna do that?' spluttered the alarmed gang boss.

'That ain't no concern of mine.'

Garvey decided to play a new tack. 'Now let's not be too hasty, Nevado,' he whined, holding up his hands in a gesture of reconciliation. 'Tell you what. I'll pay double. Give me one hour and the money will be in your bank account.' Garvey took out a pocket watch and flipped open the cover. 'Go and have a drink downstairs.' He studied the time. 'Come back at noon and we'll talk about this some more. What d'yuh say then? Is it a deal?'

Nevado wasn't listening. The blood had drained from his face. Grey eyes bulged wide, staring fixedly at the gold-plated timepiece, its unmistakable melody still resonating inside his head.

This couldn't be happening. Never for one minute had he reckoned on coming across the twin to the watch now secreted about his own person. Yet there it was, no more than three feet away.

As if from a distance, the echoing cadence of Wade Garvey's imploring suggestion filtered through the grey mist clouding his thoughts.

He repeated the offer. 'Stay and see this through and I'll also give you a hefty bonus. Can't say fairer than that, can I?'

The chiming had ceased, the watch tucked away in Garvey's vest pocket.

But the memories remained, dazzling in their intensity, as vivid now as they were at the time.

# TWELVE

## NIGHTMARE AT TUMBLEDOWN

Stanley Black had been into town. At the beginning of each month, he rode the ten miles to Cedar Springs for the purpose of buying in essential supplies. It was a hot and humid day with dark rain clouds threatening to unleash their load. After going round the various mercantiles, Stanley was ready for a drink or two. Not merely to assuage his thirst, but to garner some Dutch courage.

He had been making eyes at Cara Franklin on his last two visits, and now reckoned it was time to push for a more solid base to their relationship. Cara helped her aunt run the local dressmaker's store. She had returned his amorous looks with coy *hauteur* that Stanley had interpreted as being a positive sign. Only the briefest of communications had been possible while Cara's aunt was otherwise engaged. But it was sufficient for an understanding that they would meet up at the forthcoming barn dance.

In consequence, it was late in the day when the young man returned to the remote farmstead in West Kentucky's Tumbledown Valley. A deep rumble of thunder over Hickory Ridge presaged the arrival of an imminent downpour. But Stanley's mind was elsewhere. A dreamy smile was pasted across his youthful visage as he nonchalantly sucked on a stick of striped candy. Even when the first heavy drops of rain slapped at his old slouch hat, he failed to notice that things were not as they should be on the farm.

Cows wandering idly across the yard had not been milked. Squawking chickens were running hither and thither when they ought to be penned up. The barn door was wide open, creaking and flapping in the strengthening wind.

Most significant, however, was the body of Duke splayed out in the middle of the yard. The old guy was clearly dead, his normally luxuriant coat stained black with dried blood. It was the sight of the golden retriever that jolted the youngster from his mooning reverie.

A clap of thunder overhead echoed loudly in his ears sounding like an omen of disaster. Something had gone badly wrong.

'Pa!' he shouted above the booming drumroll. 'You there, Pa?'

A harsh crackle of forked lightning was the sole response.

Stepping down from off the wagon seat, Stanley rapidly came to the conclusion that bad deeds were afoot. He rushed into the two-roomed farmhouse praying that his mother would be there to castigate him for being late home and grumbling that his supper was cold.

'I'm home, Ma!'

No answer.

The house was empty. A cold chill rippled through his slender frame. The place had been ransacked. everything strewn about all over the place. A tornado could not have been more destructive.

So where was everybody? What did it all mean? His mind was in a quandary.

It was the intermittent banging of the barn door that caught his attention. Ignoring the driving rain, Stanley forced his stubborn legs into motion. The yard was fast assuming the consistency of a quagmire.

He felt certain that the barn would provide the answer. As if on cue, the door swung open slowly as he approached, a lightning flash outlining a hideously brutal scene resurrected from the very bowels of Hell.

Stanley gasped, his parched throat constricted by the awful shock that now faced him. He sank to his knees, desperately trying to draw breath into his cramped lungs. The sight that faced him was mesmerizing, hypnotic in its gruesome reality.

Walter Black's unconscious body hung from an overhead beam suspended by his pinioned arms. As his lacerated body twisted round, the abhorent sever-

ity of his injuries became hideously apparent. The
sight dragged a bestial cry of anguish from Stanley's
shuddering body. Bloody strips of peeled flesh hung
off the flayed back where a deadly bullwhip had cut
down to the bone.

Stanley swayed. Barely able to comprehend what
had happened, his head drooped on to his heaving
chest.

What had these animals wanted that had caused
them to commit such a barbarous atrocity?

He forced himself to look again at the butchered
carcass that had once been a vibrant human being.
That's when he noticed a slight movement of the
head. Was he seeing things? A demonic illusion sent
from Hell to torment his crazed mind?

Then, as if in slow motion, the puffy lips opened,
trying to speak. It was no figment of his fevered imag-
ination. His father really was still clinging on to life,
however tenuously.

Fresh hope coursed through Stanley's trembling
frame. Leaping up, he hurried over and cut through
the hemp rope with his pocket knife and gently
lowered the shattered body to the ground. The rising
wind howled through gaps in the barn walls like a
tormented banshee.

'Pa! Pa!' Stanley cried, whilst cradling the dying
man in his arms. Up close it was clear that unless
Walter Black received medical attention soon he
would surely die. But he had to know the truth.
'What happened? Who did this to you?'

A dry croak emerged from his father's bleeding

116

lips. Stanley ran outside and returned soon after with a dipper filled with water. The cooling liquid appeared to revive the older man, his incoherent burbling slowly resolving itself into a hoarse rasp as Walter's arm pointed to the right.

'Your mother! Check on Martha, Son!'

Stanley stood up and cautiously approached the stall indicated by his father. What he found there was more than flesh and blood could bear. How could things get any worse?

He wanted to cry out, but no sound emerged: to shed tears, but he was too stunned. The bad dreams and nightmares of his youth had nothing on this.

Martha Black had been raped, her discarded body skewered to the dirt floor by a pitchfork.

The distraught young man silently removed the grizzly object of her demise and placed a horse blanket over the body.

Returning to his father, he assured the older man that his wife was sleeping. No way could he reveal the truth. A blank regard registered none of the turmoil churning his guts into mincemeat.

Walter gave a nod of satisfaction, his bruised features composing themselves into a languid smile.

Then haltingly, he revealed the grizzly tale.


A gang of six men had ridden into the yard and demanded fresh horses and vittles for their onward journey. From their shifty-eyed appearance it was clear to Walter Black that they were outlaws on the run. Their leader was a heavy-set jasper with a black heard, his fractious mood indicating that the gang's lawless activities had not been very lucrative.

One thing he had noticed was that every one of the hard-nosed villains was sporting a red sash around his leg. Being a lone farmer, Walter had felt obliged to go along with the gang's demands that his wife cook them a meal. But when one of them noticed the gold watch chain and the equally valuable timepiece in his vest pocket, events had quickly taken a nasty turn.

While two of his henchmen had grabbed Walter pinning him against the wall, the leader had commandeered the watch.

'Now ain't this a fancy piece of goods,' he smirked flicking open the lid and grinning broadly as the musical rendition tinkled merrily. 'Must be worth a tidy sum.'

'Couple of hundred bucks at least,' voiced a thin wiry critter going under the unlikely handle of Ten Gallon Brewster on account of his over-sized hat.

The remark elicited a gruff response from the farmer. 'It's a family heirloom and not worth a bean in the way of hard cash.' The bearded outlaw leader uttered a manic snarl. His rabid anger was given weight by a heavy back-hander that sent the poor recipient sprawling on the dirt floor.

'Don't give me that. Think I'm some kinda greenhorn?' he hollered angrily jabbing a finger at the shiny bauble. 'I know solid gold when I see it. And this little beauty tells me you ain't no hard-up dirt farmer like you're tryin' to make us believe.'

'That means there must be a heap more like it around here,' cut in one of the gang greedily scanning the interior of the farmhouse.

'Just what I was thinkin', Jack,' replied the leader. 'So where yuh hidin' all the spoils, fella?'

'I'm telling you there ain't nothing here worth the bother,' pleaded Walter with mounting fear behind his haunted eyes.

'Do you believe that, boys?' asked the big man of his cohorts.

They all sniggered at the suggestion.

'Not a chance, boss,' was the scoffing reaction.

'Get him over to the barn,' ordered the leader. Here was his chance of some easy pickings following the disastrous bank hold up at Boarman's Creek. 'There's more space over there for us to persuade this turkey where his best interests lie.'

The implied threat to his health was not lost on Walter Black.

'Please mister,' he begged. 'Look around you. Is this the home of a wealthy landowner? I can barely make ends meet.'

'Just the way for a crafty bastard to conceal the family fortune, I'd say,' ranted the outlaw as he manhandled Walter across the farmyard. 'Safer than the First National Bank vault in St Louis.'

At that point, Stanley placed a finger over his father's cracked lips. He didn't need to hear any more. It was brutally obvious what had happened next.

'The gang leader put a bullet in my hide once

he'd had his fun . . . when it was obvious there was going to be no . . . . no treasure trove forthcoming.' The narration had exhausted Walter Black. He panted harshly from the exertion. 'Must have figured I was dead.'

'What I can't understand is why they never set fire to the place,' frowned Stanley dribbling more water down his father's parched throat. 'They must have been good and riled up on learning there was gonna be no pot of gold at the end of the rainbow.'

Briefly rallying, the farmer was able to voice his opinion. 'One of the redlegs kept urging the boss to leave . . . said they needed to get on the trail. The skunks knew that smoke from a fire would have attracted unwelcome attention from the posse on their tail.'

A racking cough seized hold of the elder Black's innards. Blood dribbled from his mouth. Then his watery eyes closed. His shattered body trembled convulsively. Dark clouds had dulled the light inside the barn to a turbid grey. A throaty rumble from on high proclaimed the imminent arrival of a new soul into the Heavenly host.

Walter Black had milked his final cow.

Stanley's face paled to a deathly mask of hate. There was no forgiveness in his heart, no turning of the other cheek like the preacher always ranted on about of a Sunday.

And there never would be. Not until this cowardly attack on his kin had been avenged.

He buried his parents beside the grave of his

younger sister who had died of the fever the previous summer. Even though his mother had been an avid church-goer, assiduously reading her Bible every night, Stanley felt no sense of peace, only a profound sense of grieving that could only be assuaged by the eradication of the cancer that had been its cause.

His life's mission from here on would he to that end.

Although the rain had stopped, a chill wind played a mournful tune amid the swaying branches of the lone cottonwood overshadowing the graves.

Out of respect for his mother's beliefs, he removed his hat and whispered a few words over the graves. It was the least he could do. Then, taking out the gold watch, the twin of his father's, that had been presented on his twenty-first birthday, Stanley opened it up. The dulcet chimes gave out a soulful lament that echoed round the tiny graveyard.

A flight of cactus wrens ceased their chirruping as if they sensed the young man's distress. Only the mournful howl of a distant lone coyote lent credence to the grim proceedings.

Stanley had always been adept with a long gun, a necessity on the remote homestead in order to bring fresh meat to the family table. But he had never carried a handgun. That was about to change. The only one in the house was an old cap and ball Remington stuck above the fireplace gathering dust.

It would be a start.

There was no knowing where or how it would end.

In company with a Sharps breechloader and the

Remington, Stanley Black left Tumbledown Valley. He vowed only to return when the killings had been avenged.

# THIRTEEN

# CHANGE OF HEART

That had been fifteen years ago.

And Stanley Black was now the renowned gunfighter who went by the name of Nevado. His quest for revenge on the killers of his parents had become like the fabled El Dorado. Still a yearning that occasionally surfaced when some reminder nudged his subconscious, otherwise it lay dormant. The years of fruitless searching had taken their toil. And just like those old-timers who dreamed about discovering that legendary pot of gold, he now had little hope of ever achieving the justice that had eaten at his heart for so long.

Could he really be nearing the end of his pursuit?

It barely seemed possible after riding down so many box canyons, galloping off on endless wild goose chases. Yet there was the evidence staring him in the face, the irrefutable proof that Wade Garvey had committed the unpardonable acts against his parents.

Ace Montana and Mace Foggerty were the only other henchmen in the office. Neither appeared to have sensed the anguish threatening to erupt from the hired gunfighter.

Quickly Nevado shook off the crushing weight of despondency that had threatened to overwhelm him. With a supreme effort of willpower, he held his bursting temper in check. His whole body tingled. The blood rising in his veins turned his swarthy features the shade of a ripe tomato.

But the sight and sound of his father's chiming timepiece had been a rude shock to the system.

'Kinda warm in here,' he muttered, dabbing a neckcloth across his sweating forehead. 'I need some air.' He lurched over to a window and heaved up the sash breathing deeply.

Garvey accorded him a quizzical scowl. 'You OK, Nevado?' he questioned, thick eyebrows raised. 'You look a bit groggy.'

'Musta been some'n I ate,' he said quickly rallying his thoughts. This would never do. He needed to figure out some way of turning this course of events to his advantage before the gang boss put two and two together.

Although it was barely more than a long minute since Garvey had suggested a new deal, it seemed like his whole life had passed before his eyes.

'Maybe I was a little hasty,' Nevado averred forcing his icy gaze away from the gang leader's vest pocket.

'Patch was right. I am close to solving the case. The reason I wanted to pull out?' A menacing gleam had appeared in the gunfighter's eyes. 'My pa sent me a cable saying he needs help to . . . lay some ghosts to rest.'

'What's that supposed to mean?' queried the bemused Garvey. 'You sure are actin' strange, mister.'

Nevado laughed. 'Don't mind me,' he said. 'Family stuff, that's all.'

'Well you sort out this business rapid like, and you can chase after as many ghosts as you want with my blessing.'

'Just got a few more lines of inquiry to pursue, then I can set the trap that's going to catch the biggest durned rat of them all.' Nevado's cool demeanour had set granite hard. His mouth twisted in a warped leer that spoke of frosty resolution as he swung on his heel and left the room.

'That guy gives me the shivers,' muttered Ace Montana. 'I'll be glad when this town's shut of him.'

'Just so long as he earns his bonus,' rapped Garvey, extracting a cigar and lighting up. 'Then maybe we can carry out a little haunting of our own and magic that dough back into our pockets.'

A manic chortle rumbled in Mace Foggerty's throat.

'Now that's some'n I can't wait to see,' he chuntered.

Figuring that Garvey might have him watched, Nevada returned to the Imperial and retired to his room. He had much to think on, plans that needed making. There was a tight knot in his guts as he thought of what had to be done. And Aaron Spedding had earned the right to be a central part of Wade Garvey's final débâcle.

By the time he had figured it all out, darkness had fallen.

The shadows of night blurred his image as he skirted behind the buildings fronting Main Street. A dim light shone in the second-floor back room of the barber's. Spedding was doubtless on tenterhooks wondering where his future lay; whether the county lawyers would back his claim against Wade Garvey, or try him for cold-blooded murder.

It would come as a shock to hear of the vital role he was to play in bringing down the gang boss.

Nevado flung a small pebble at the window. Following a brief interval, the sash was raised to reveal a flushed countenance. The barber had clearly been knocking back the hard stuff as if it were going out of fashion.

'Who's there?' The words were slurred, the staring eyes bloodshot.

Nevado scowled. This was the last thing he needed.

'Let me in!' he demanded without preamble. This guy would need to be stone cold sober if he was to be of any use in the forthcoming action.

'Oh, it's you,' answered Spedding with little enthusiasm, and more than a hint of trepidation. 'Better come on up, the door's on the latch.'

Once ensconced in the barber's living quarters, Nevado wasted no time in brewing up a pot of strong coffee which he then proceeded to pour down the little guy's throat.

It took a long hour. But the potent fusion of Grade Five Arbuckles and the realization that he was receiving a welcome if unexpected reprieve, speeded up the sobering process.

'What made you change your mind?' muttered the incredulous barber whilst imbibing his fifth mug of coffee. 'I was convinced that you'd have left town by now.'

'Turns out we both have a lot in common where that skunk is concerned.' Barely suppressed anger edged the brusquely delivered comment.

'How d'you mean?'

Nevado slowly extracted the gold watch from his pocket, placed it reverently on the table, then flicked open the lid. The plaintive rendition trilled melodically.

When it finally stopped, a heavy quietude enfolded the close atmosphere in the room. Spedding understood that this was one period when silence was indeed golden. His associate would reveal all in his own good time.

It was five minutes before the white-haired gunfighter felt sufficiently composed enough to open up his heart.

'So I'm going to need your help to pull off the plan I have in mind,' he said following the grim revelation. 'But one thing I ask,' he finished, 'is that you leave Garvey to me.'

The little man balked at that notion.

'What gives you the right to finish off the rat?' he retorted, hackles rising. 'Ain't I got just cause?'

Nevado admonished the barber with a chastening frown of disapproval.

'A man can get so's he enjoys killing,' he cautioned with a serious hint of rebuke. 'It gets into his blood. Before long, he can't stop. Just like with the drink.' He held the little man's gaze meaningfully. 'The taking of a human life is not something to be undertaken lightly. Every man I've terminated has destroyed a bit of me in the process. And once Garvey's out of the picture, I'm gonna hang up my guns and settle down some place far away from here.'

'Back in Kentucky maybe?'

'Maybe.'

'Guess you're right about the taking of life,' Spedding added with thoughtful deliberation while sipping his coffee. A look of acquiescence drifted across his rounded features. 'Each time I sharpened the razor, there was a sickly churning in my guts at what I was doing, but there was also a buzz of exhilaration, excitement even.'

He purposefully omitted to inform his *compadre* that where Wade Garvey was concerned, he had his own agenda to fill.

Unwittingly, Nevado responded with a satisfied nod of approval. Then he proceeded to outline the plan he had in mind.

'Do you have a rifle?' he finished.

The barber shook his head. 'Never had need of one before.'

'Well you do now!' chided Nevado. Then with an apathetic shrug added, 'Never mind. I'll provide the hardware.'

The scheme involved a couple of sticks of dynamite and fuses which could only he acquired by breaking into Fred Tanner's general store. At the same time, Nevado would purloin a rifle and ammunition for his associate. This would have to be done after the store had closed for the night and Tanner had gone home. It was a lucky break that the store was a lock-up and the owner lived elsewhere.

At around ten o'clock, Nevado left the barber's upstairs room reminding him that they were to meet up the following afternoon at 1 p.m. Their liaison was to be at the rear of the new house under construction adjoining that owned by Wade Garvey.

It was now Friday so the building workers would finish for the weekend at noon the following day. By one o'clock the site would be empty.

Nobody to disturb them.

It was a warm night as Nevado ambled along the boardwalk. His destination took him past the Imperial where Penny Wilson was taking the air before retiring for the night. The light cast by a street lantern caught the sensuous planes of her alabaster complexion. The sight was enough to set Nevado's pulse racing.

Neither had spoken since their previously less

than cordial split.

'I'll be leaving soon,' he said abruptly. 'My work here is just about complete. But I would strongly advise you to stay indoors tomorrow afternoon.'

Penny's eyes lifted. The revelation came as a complete surprise. And she realized that much as she disapproved of the gunfighter's way of life, she could not get him out of her system. This was not what she wanted to hear.

'What are you aiming to do?' Concern impinged itself into the soft folds of her fearful regard.

'Best you don't know,' he replied. 'Let's just say I've reached the end of a long road, and there's a price to be paid.'

A wry smile crossed the darkened crevices of his face. Then without further comment he hurried away, disappearing into the Stygian gloom.

# FOURTEEN

# SHANGRI-LA

Even though Saturday was his busiest day, Aaron had closed up early. Pinning a sign on to the salon door, he claimed it was due to illness. Then he left by the rear door of the premises taking a circuitous route behind Main Street to avoid any unwanted encounters.

At 12.50 p.m. he sidled up behind a pile of rough planking adjacent to the half-finished house up the shallow grade known as Nob Hill on the outskirts of town. Maintaining a low profile, he cast a wary peeper across the intervening dirt roadway to the recently finished residence now occupied by Wade Garvey.

The finest craftsmen had been brought in to design an abode that reflected the gang boss's aspirations. Its ostentatious flamboyance indicated to all and sundry that Wade Garvey was a successful businessman. He had purposely ensured that the house was built at the top of a hill overlooking Buckeye where he could play at being king of the castle by naming it Shangri-La.

On the same stretch of road, but much lower down, were other houses owned by the prominent citizens of Buckeye. None had any of the garish pretensions espoused by Garvey's residence.

The house appeared to be empty.

Garvey would be at the Texas Belle, doubtless rubbing his grubby hands in anticipation of the imminent showcase trial of a serial killer. Aaron smiled. He was in for the shock of his life.

That was when he perceived a face at one of the downstairs windows. It was Chocktaw Pete. The half-breed must have been left on guard. Quickly ducking down behind the planking, the barber was joined by his newly acquired partner. Nevado had also noted the Indian's unwelcome presence.

'We need to take that varmint out,' he announced.

'How we gonna do that?'

Nevado considered this dilemma for a minute before replying.

'You call on the turkey and say that Garvey wants him down at the Belle pronto,' he explained. 'Tell him there's big trouble afoot. A dumbass like that is unlikely to question you. Soon as he comes outside, I'll slug him.' He gave the barber a questioning look. 'Got that?'

The little man concurred, although it was clear as a crystal lake to the gunfighter that his associate was undeniably nervous regarding the forthcoming showdown. He was like a fish out of water, and twitchy as a Mexican jumping bean.

The gunfighter stifled an overspill of irritation.

'You OK with this?' he asked in a more conciliatory tone.

Aaron wiped the sweat from his face and squared his round shoulders. Tight-lipped with steely determination he replied with a terse nod of his bullet head.

'As ever!' was the brittle response.

'Then give me five minutes to circle around the back of the house,' said Nevado. 'Soon as you get my signal, make your move.'

With that he disappeared across the back lot. Fleeting glimpses of a grey flannel shirt in the harsh sunlight found Aaron once again sweating like a pig – and not on account of the burning heat.

It seemed like an hour before he caught sight of his partner peeping round the front porch of Shangri-La. A raised hand informed him that his moment of death or glory had arrived.

Sucking in a deep breath, he emerged from concealment and edged out into the open. Tense nerve ends strung tight as a drumskin, he expected a bullet in the guts at any moment.

It never came.

Girding his loins he called out to the man inside the house. His voice sounded remote, as if it belonged elsewhere, in some netherworld. It emerged as barely more than a hoarse rasp. He coughed, clearing his throat and spitting a globule of phlegm into the dust.

'Anybody in there?' he repeated, in a more explicit and confident manner. 'I've got a message here from Wade Garvey.'

The curtains moved but there was no response to the summons.

'I know you're in there, Pete,' he hollered. 'And Mr Garvey won't like it if'n you ignore his orders.'

That appeared to do the trick. Even a stony-faced jughead like Chocktaw Pete would hesitate to refuse an order issued by the formidable gang boss.

The front door opened, slowly but with infinite caution. The weathered face of the half-breed appeared, a suspicious glower pasted across the mahogany façade.

'What this about?' Chocktaw Pete was no word-smith.

'Mr Garvey wants you down at the saloon.'

'Why?'

'It's all in this message.' Aaron held out a slip of paper.

Nevado smiled. Nice touch. The barber had figured out the best means of getting the Indian out of the house. And it had worked.

Pete stepped across the broad veranda offering his back to the gunfighter. Silent as a wraith, Nevado padded across the intervening walkway and laid his drawn pistol across the Indian's exposed head.

Pete went down like a sack of coal.

'Help me get him out of sight,' ordered Nevado.

134

By the time they had manhandled the Indian's ungainly body over to the building site, he had partially regained consciousness.

Spedding was all for getting his razor in on the action. The lethal blade glinted in the sunlight. Pete's eyes bulged. It was only Nevado's restraining hand that prevented another blood-letting.

'What you playing at?' he snapped acidly. 'Didn't nothing I said last night stay in that head of your'n?'

'He's one of Garvey's scumbags. So he deserves to die.' The statement was laid down in a callous even vein, cold-blooded and devoid of feeling.

'Let me ask you this, Aaron,' Nevado enquired firmly, whilst maintaining a tight hold of the barber's razor hand. 'Was an Indian involved in the dark deeds that took out your kin?'

'I guess not.'

'Nor mine. So Chocktaw Pete lives. Savvy?' The gunfighter's iron-hard gaze held that of his companion. 'All the others will have to take their chances.'

Spedding's resistance was resolute but short-lived. He soon wilted under the brittle regard, snapping the cut-throat shut.

'Agreed,' he muttered. But the evil grimace he shot at the Indian did not bode well for the redman's future health.

'We'll hogtie and gag him. That way he won't be no trouble,' said Nevado breathing easier. This little guy was a wolf in sheep's clothing, a regular mean-eyed cuss. He would need watching.

Chocktaw Pete looked on anxiously during the

scrappy exchange. His understanding of the white-man's language may have been limited, but there was no mistaking who was on his side this time around. If he ever succeeded in getting free, that thought would not be forgotten.

Once the Indian had been removed from the drama, Nevado announced that it was time for the main performance to begin.

He showed the barber how to use a Winchester repeater with its lever action and the lateral cartridge ejector. Secreting him on the upper floor of the half-finished structure, Nevado emphasized the salient grounds for holding fire until he gave the signal.

'I aim to give them the chance to surrender—'

Spedding cut him short with an indignant rejoinder. 'After all we've suffered, and you're wanting to let the bastards off the hook? How could you even consider such a notion?'

'It's Garvey and Patch that I want,' Nevado stressed, his tone palpably hardening. 'The others are just hired hands, probably weren't even there at the time.'

'How can you be so sure of that?'

'I can't,' he concurred. 'But don't you think there's been enough killing already?' His remark was aimed specifically at the barber's most recent activities with a cut-throat razor. 'If they back off, we let them ride out. Garvey and Patch will stand trial.'

'And what if they get off?' Spedding was still not convinced.

'Then, and only then. . . .' He paused willing the

barber to accept his reasoning. 'I go after them with all guns blazing. So what d'you say?'

The barber was not convinced and knew exactly how he was going to play out his hand. No way was he going to let some conniving lawyer spoil his moment of retribution. But he kept such ideas under wraps. An icy calm had smoothed out all the tense lines on his puffy face. The steady, even regard gave nothing away.

'You're right, of course,' he iterated with a blithe nod of the head. 'We'll play it your way.'

'You'll see. It's the right thing to do.' Nevado evinced a deep sigh of relief. Then proceeded to outline the next phase of his plan.

'Remember,' he emphasized, 'You only let that Winchester do the talking if they refuse to play ball.'

Spedding replied with a curt nod.

Satisfied, Nevado hustled over to Shangri-La and positioned the sticks of dynamite where they would achieve the maximum effect. Spedding watched carefully as he unravelled a spool of fuse wire, backing towards the building site ensuring that the delicate wire did not snag on any obstructions.

Satisfied that all was in place, he called to the barber in the room above. 'Keep your head down, Aaron. This is gonna make one helluva bang.'

Fastening the wire ends to the detonator, the gunfighter raised the plunger and held his breath.

Two seconds.

Three.

A final intake of breath and he pressed down hard.

There was a brief sizzle as the connection was made. Then nothing. Something had gone wrong: a broken joint, unreliable dynamite. A whole heap of reasons flashed through his brain.

All were forgotten as a mighty explosion ripped through the house. The ground shook with fury as Shangri-La was ripped apart. Glass windows exploded outwards. Flames quickly took hold, licking at the solid oak supports that still remained intact. Dust and debris scattered in all directions pummelling the building site where the two ambushers were concealed.

The devastating result was more than Nevado could have hoped for. He couldn't restrain a caterwauling cheer of acclamation.

'Yahooogh!!' he yelped gleefully. 'Now ain't that some'n!'

Even Aaron Spedding was caught unawares. Not in his wildest dreams had he ever expected such a prodigious outcome. All he could do was stare openmouthed, ogling the inferno that, moments before, had displayed all the trappings of a splendid mansion.

It was Nevado who snapped out of the spellbinding mood first.

'Get ready!' he hollered, settling himself behind the palisade of wood stanchions. 'Won't be long now. And remember how we're gonna play this.'

There was no reply.

# FIFTEEN

# GUNFIGHT AT
# NOB HILL

Garvey was in the midst of a poker game. Ace
Montana was the dealer. A couple more diehard
gamblers were avidly studying their own hands.
Thick tendrils of cigar smoke rose like twisted
serpents towards the yellowed ceiling. The dim interior was hazily illuminated by an oily tallow lamp
hanging over the green baize table.

Everything as normal in the Texas Belle.

The abrupt explosion took them all by surprise.
Even at this distance from the source, the tremor
could be felt beneath their feet.

'What in thunderation was that?' ejaculated
Montana dropping the cards. Everybody in the
saloon ceased their activities and angled wary
peepers towards the open door.

'Sounded mighty like an explosion to me,' piped up an old miner standing at the bar. 'That's dynamite if ever I heard it,' he added, with a sagacious curl of the lip.

Wade Garvey leapt to his feet. This had bad news stamped all over it.

Quickly regaining his composure, he snapped an order to the hovering Jack Patch. 'Get all the boys together. I don't like the sound of this.'

At that precise moment, Shifty Cornwell lumbered through the batwings shouting, 'It's the Shangri-La, boss.'

'What about it?'

'Gone up like a Thanksgiving Day bonfire.'

The outlaw's blunt remark hit Garvey with sledge-hammer force. But he soon recovered from the stupefying news. Under fire, Wade Garvey had always been able to make a effective counter attack. It was one reason why he had become a respected leader of men. This was no exception.

His initial thought was for Chocktaw Pete who was house guard for the day, not with any philanthropic concern in mind. He automatically assumed that the red devil had fallen asleep on the job.

'Get your weapons, boys,' he snarled, checking the load on his revolver. 'And bring plenty of ammo. Somebody's out to supplant my position in this town. And I reckon I know who it is.'

Jack Patch pre-empted Garvey's declaration with his own cutting remark. 'Has to be that skunk Nevado. You should never have brought him in, Wade.'

Garvey cursed at his lieutenant's retort which was especially painful because he recognized it to be well founded.

A further ten minutes was needed for the whole gang, or what was left of them, to gather outside the saloon. All arrived fully armed and ready.

'Spread out on either side of the street,' ordered Garvey, a Henry carbine cradled across his chest. 'And keep your eyes peeled. This Nevado can be as cunning as a snake in the grass.'

At the edge of town they turned up Nob Hill. It was no more than 200 yards up the shallow grade to where his beloved Shangri-La had once stood. Witnessing the place in total ruins, smoke billowing from the blackened husk, was almost too much for the tough hardcase.

His pace faltered, hard flinty eyes watering with despair.

Somebody was going to pay dearly for this. Shrugging off the bleak lassitude that had threatened to engulf him, Garvey squared his shoulders. A grim determination to exact his own brand of vengeance on the perpetrators hustled to the fore.

Barring his way forward at the junction of Main and Nob stood Hoot Cresswell. 'I don't want a blood-bath in my town, Wade,' he said trying to inject some fire into his utterance. 'Let me send for the county sheriff and we can deal with this in a proper legal manner.'

Coming to a standstill facing the marshal, Garvey accorded his hired lawdog a sneer of contempt.

141

'Remember who pays your bonus, Hoot,' he growled.
'I can get rid of you any time I choose. So just step
out of the way and I'll forget this little hiccup ever
took place.'

'Can't do that, Wade. I swore to uphold the law in
Buckeye.' Cresswell's reply was stilted and nervous.
'Sure, I let you have your own way on a number of
issues, but this is my job: so let me handle it.'

'Gotten yourself a conscience, Hoot?' spat Jack
Patch pushing forward.

'Some'n like that maybe,' returned the lawman
drawing himself up to his full height.

'Well it's too late for all that hogwash.'

Without further ado, the outlaw drew his pistol
and pumped the whole chamber into the marshal's
bulky torso. Garvey merely grunted. Stepping
forward, he pushed the quivering hulk aside and
continued slowly up the hill.

'What were those shots?' enquired Nevado, who
was unable to see the action being played out at the
bottom of the hill.

'Looks like the marshal was trying to make a
stand,' replied Spedding with a touch of respect in
his voice.

'How did it go?'

'He failed.'

Once the approaching private army had come to
within fifty yards of the burning conflagration,
Nevado chose that moment to reveal himself. Only
his head was visible above the layers of planking, just
in case things went awry.

142

'Hold it right there, Garvey,' he called.

'That you, Whitey?' snarled the gang boss levering the carbine and dropping down on to one knee. 'You know that you don't stand a chance of getting out of here alive.'

From the blunt statement, Nevado knew that Garvey had no intention of backing off. This was a fight to the death. But he still had hopes that the hired hands might see sense and not want to risk getting their heads shot off just to mollify the boss's pride.

'You fellas down there,' he called. 'Why don't you all just turn around and ride off. This is no fight of your'n. It's between me and Garvey. Not forgetting Mr Patch, of course. Why give yourselves a dose of lead poisoning for a pair of—'

His attempt at reasoning with the gang was inter-rupted by a stream of invective from over his head. It ended with the barber announcing proudly, 'I'm the one who you've all been so shit scared of. Me, the meek and mild barber of Buckeye.' The stunning declaration was followed by an deranged howl of laughter. 'Don't yuh find that funny, boys? Ain't yuh gonna laugh?'

Nevado was impotent to do anything. All he could do was listen to the manic ranting. The guy was losing his marbles, cracking up under the strain.

That was when Spedding decided to give full vent to his fury by opening up with the Winchester. Nevado cursed aloud. Just when he might have been able to reduce the odds on their survival by a substantial margin, the goddamned barber's outburst was threatening the whole scheme.

Now they were in for an all out gun battle.

'Scatter, boys,' hollered Garvey as the first shots rang out. 'This critter is tryin' to play us for a bunch of suckers. The man who brings me the scalp of either one of these bastards will earn hisself a thousand-dollar bonus.'

Luckily for the outlaws, the barber's greenhorn gunplay had meant that all the shots had gone well wide of the mark.

'Now that you've gone and unleashed a hornet's next,' harangued the irate gunfighter. 'Make every shot count.'

For the next half-hour, the air was filled with flying lead. Secreted at a more elevated level with good cover, the advantage was with Nevado and his partner. He had managed to wing Ace Montana in the shoulder when the gambler tried to move up closer. That left six others including the two main adversaries, neither of whom was making his presence felt. At least Chocktaw Pete had been removed from the equation.

In the upper room of the half-finished dwelling, the barber had slowly but surely found the range and improved his accuracy with the Winchester.

A strident yell of delight followed his next volley of shots as Shifty Cornwell threw up his arms and collapsed in a heap.

'Got one of the bastards.'

After an hour, the firing had dropped to a more

desultory level. Nevado had taken note that Mace
Foggerty had been sent hack into town, no doubt to
acquire fresh ammunition. There was no such advantage for the two antagonists. Indeed, it was becoming
readily apparent that they were trapped up here with
no place to go.

He felt a simmering resentment against the
unhinged barber, but he couldn't really blame the
guy after all these years. Nevado also wanted justice.
But as a professional gunman, he was able to keep a
lid on his bloodlust.

'Don't waste any shells, Aaron,' he advised. 'If'n
we run out, it's curtains for the both of us.' He waited
for a reponse but a heavy silence hung over the
battleground like a mourning quilt. 'You hear me,
mister?'

Then he saw Chocktaw Pete sneeking behind a
cluster of rocks over to his right. The 'breed must
have worked himself free.

So what of Aaron Spedding?

A macabre thought occured to him that the
Indian had exacted his own form of retribution on
the little man who had been all set to slit his gizzard.
He turned round, all set to mount the stairs to the
upper storey, when a glint of steel caught the edge of
his vision.

Stuck into a wooden paling less than a yard from
his face was the barber's revered cut-throat. Smeared
in blood, it was a clear sign from the Indian that he
could quite easily have terminated Nevado's oxygen
intake as well. Realizing how close he had come to

strumming with the angels, the gunfighter shuddered as the grim reaper laughed in his face.

And that meant Garvey had one more brigand at his disposal. It now occurred to the gunfighter that maybe this hadn't been such a good idea after all. Perhaps he should have destroyed Garvey's house while the skunk was inside.

Too late for personal recriminations now. He was a man alone, fighting against the forces of repellent evil with a double reason for ensuring that retribution was meted out in full measure.

Breaking into his morbid reflections, a trenchant shout came from down the hill.

'You ready to give yourself up, Nevado?' called Garvey during a period of relative quiet. 'Pete tells me that he's evened up the score with that little rat Spedding. And Jack here reckons he can take you any time. Man-to-man. A duel to the finish. What d'yuh say? Winner rides out unscathed.'

Nevado didn't believe a word of it. As soon as he showed himself, he would be cut down in a hail of lead.

Then he remembered.

Inside his haversack – had he packed two or three sticks of dynamite? With uncertain hesitation, he reached inside the canvas bag, his fingers tentatively searching. And there it was. Removing the all important stick, he also discovered a small piece of fuse wire. It would provide no more than five seconds' leeway. That would have to be sufficent.

Following the return of Mace Foggerty and the

ammunition, Nevado realized that it was only a matter of time before they rushed him. He might gun down a couple, but then it would be all over. Garvey now knew that only the hired gunfighter lay between himself and a clean bill of health.

With careful yet swift deliberation, Nevado forced the fuse into the soft head of the explosive concoction. He scraped a vesta against his pants and applied the small flame to the fuse. It sizzled loudly. Arm stretched out behind, he flung the deadly serpent down Nob Hill.

Over and over it spun, spitting and hissing like an angry sidewinder. Five, six seconds. . . . Then it happened.

The earth-shattering detonation shook the foundations of the half-finished house. It creaked and rocked alarmingly, hung in the air briefly, then crumpled into a chaotic heap of detritus. Nevado flung himself to one side, rolling frantically to avoid the jumbled disarray of broken timbers.

Swirling skeins of yellow dust blotted out the afternoon sun creating an eerie twilight world.

Nevado understood that this was his last chance to take the survivors of the explosion by surprise. Drawing the .44 Colt Frontier, he quickly ejected the spent shells and thumbed fresh loads into the chambers from his denuded shellbelt. There were only four bullets left.

Ratcheting the hammer to full cock, he scampered down the hill, hawkish eyes piercing the gloom for signs of life.

Mace Foggerty staggered towards him. The outlaw was disorientated and bleeding from a scalp wound.

'Drop your hardware, Mace,' ordered Nevado. 'This is the end of the line.'

Such a course of action was anathema to all hardened gunnies. Foggerty was no exception. Instantly on the alert, a growl of rage emerged from the outlaw's dust-caked visage.

'No chance, Snowball!' he yammered, going for his shooting iron. It cleared leather but not before a single bullet slammed into his forehead punching him back. He hit the hard ground with a thud and remained still.

Further down the hill, the gunfighter came across the bodies of two more Garvey men. Ace Montana and Shifty Cornwell were both dead. As the dust-cloud thinned, Nevado widened his search, ever watchful of an ambush.

But there was no sign of either Garvey or his lieutenant.

Nevado let out a stream of epithets. Now he would have to flush the rats out of their holes. Wade Garvey was finished in Buckeye. But would he cut his losses and light out for pastures new?

The answer was to be found at the Texas Belle.

# SIXTEEN

# KIDNAPPED!

Main Street was deserted. The citizens of Buckeye had deemed it wise to remain indoors while the lead was flying. Not even the twitching snout of an inquisitive hound dog could be seen. Edging along the deserted boardwalk, Nevado kept his eyes peeled for any sign of retaliation. His pistol had only three shells left.

He was afforded no time to considered this limitation to his firepower as a blast cut through the static air. Splinters of wood erupted from a veranda upright only inches from his head. Spotting a crouched figure beside the dressmaker's store two blocks west, Nevado triggered off a couple of shots. Neither found its target. But he had the pleasure of seeing the bushwhacker disappearing down the alleyway. That brief sighting was enough.

The black vest and pants meant only one thing.

149

*Jack Patch!*

Hurrying down the constricted opening between the two stores immediately opposite, Nevado scurried across the back lot hoping to catch the gunman unawares and surprise him from the rear. He leapt effortlessly over a corral fence, ducking low for a quick scan of the terrain. If his supposition was correct, Patch should be somewhere close by. Noiselessly, he crept along the edge of the corral to its corner abutting a stable.

Then he saw him. Concealed behind a wagon, the outlaw had obviously been expecting his adversary to appear from the direction of Main. In consequence, he had his back facing Nevado. Eyes firmly glued to the alley entrance down which he had so recently sprinted, Patch was clearly hoping for an easy target.

Nevado holstered his pistol and carefully stepped out from the cover of the fence. He could have drilled the gunman in the back, but that was the coward's way, not that of the professional gunfighter. Gingerly he approached to within ten yards of the outlaw.

'You looking for me, Jack?'

The words, flat and devoid of emotion, sliced through the silence that had enveloped the town. Patch stiffened. Instinctively he knew what was coming. Slowly, almost catlike, he stood and swung to face his nemesis.

His narrowed gaze held that of the other man.

'So it's finally come to this then?' sighed Patch.

'One to one,' opined Nevado, watching his opponent's every move. 'Just like you always wanted. Except you figured on taking me out the bushwhacker's way.' He aimed a mocking smile at the gunman. 'Now that ain't very sporting, is it, Jack?'

Patch scowled, ignoring the barbed comment. 'Just tell me one thing,' he said.

Nevado waited.

'Blastin' poor ole Wade's pride and joy.' The outlaw emitted a harsh guffaw. 'Now that was mean-spirited, don't yuh reckon? So why d'yuh do it?'

'Family business,' Nevado rapped acidly. 'And no concern of your'n.'

The curt rebuff drew a baleful curse from the outlaw. 'OK, mister, if that's how yuh want it. Enough of the verbals. Let's get this done.' He crouched, right hand hovering above the butt of his revolver, gloved fingers flexing involuntarily.

'Suits me,' agreed Nevado, who was much less on edge than the gunman even though he only had one shot remaining. He recognized the signs, those slight telling nuances that told him the exact moment his adversary was about to draw. In Patch's case it was a momentary lift of his right shoulder.

An owl hooted somewhere in the distance. A group of cactus wrens twittered on a roof top with little regard for the deadly game being enacted below.

For the merest flicker of an instant, time stood still.

Then both men drew as one. Flame lanced from the two pistol barrels. But only one bullet found its mark.

It was enough.

Patch teetered uncertainly. His startled gaze dropped to the rapidly spreading patch of red on his chest. Eyes glazing over as the grim reaper came a'knocking, he slumped to his knees. One final look at his opponent, a faint smirk, then he keeled over.

'That's for you, Aaron,' muttered Nevado: the bleak weariness in his eyes implied no sense of satisfaction. Jack Patch was merely an obstacle in the way of his main protagonist.

Nevado wasted no time in idle posturing. With the practised speed of an experienced gunhand, he extracted the shells from Patch's belt and filled his own as well as the Colt Frontier.

Then he went in search of Garvey.

Entering the Texas Belle by the back door, he sidled along a dim passage and peered cautiously into the main body of the saloon. Only one man stood at the bar. Clearly in a bad way, Chocktaw Pete was clutching the handle of a knife protruding from his side.

Nevado's first thought was who could have skewered the half-breed? He was in no position to cause any trouble so Nevado hustled into the room and walked over. The bartender was idly wiping the counter, displaying no concern for the injured man.

'What happened?' Nevado asked tersely.

A rumbling growl surfaced from deep within the 'breed's inner being. It was the first time the gunfighter had seen him exhibit any form of unbridled emotion. Pete was good and angry. A simmering revulsion burned behind the slit eyes.

'Black-hearted white-eyes chief – Wade Garvey,' he hissed, spitting the name out in disgust. 'He pulling out, leaving Buckeye.' Pete couldn't contain his outburst. He obviously understood more of the white-man's tongue than he had let on. 'Caught him emptying safe upstairs. When Pete asked for his share, knife in guts was answer.' His craggy face wrinkled in pain.

'Let me take a look,' offered Nevado. Then, to the laconic barman, 'Some'n strong over here, and not that rotgut neither.' The man grudgingly complied.

After examining the Indian, Nevado gave him a reassuring smile. 'You ain't gonna peg out just yet awhile, Pete,' he said, helping the outlaw to his feet. 'It's only a flesh wound. Once the doc's sewn you up, be good as new.'

Pete eyed his unlikely benefactor with scepticism. 'Why you do this for Indian?'

Nevado responded with a noncommittal shrug.

'One good turn deserves another.' But he was more concerned now about the whereabouts of the former gang boss. 'How long ago did Garvey leave?' he asked.

'Twenty minutes only.'

'Any notion as to which direction he took?'

Pete considered the question before spewing out a sneering reply. 'Him go west. Always talking about San Francisco and Nob Hill. Wanted to be big shot dude with fancy carriage and servants.'

Nevado nodded gravely. If he left straight away, he

should be able to catch the varmint before sundown.

Having deposited the Indian with the local sawbones, Nevado had one more call to make before trailing out after Garvey.

Immediately Nevado entered the hallowed precincts of the Imperial hotel, he knew that something was wrong. Ambrose, the desk clerk, was extremely flustered, his behaviour disconcerting and incoherent. The gunfighter could extract no rational answer to his questions regarding the availability of the proprietor.

Increasingly frustrated, he was forced to terminate the fit of panic with a stiff backhander across the clerk's face. The blunt measure was enough to terminate the outburst instantly, returning the clerk to near normal lucidity.

'So where is Miss Wilson?' repeated Nevado brusquely.

'Mr Garvey came by and took her off,' he keened, arms waving like a windmill. 'Forced her to go with him at the point of a gun. When I tried to intervene, he threatened to shoot me.' This latter disclosure saw the desk clerk reverting to his previous hysterics.

But Nevado had heard enough.

He left the hotel and went in search of his cayuse which was stabled at Jackson's livery barn at the far end of Main Street. Within ten minutes he was mounted and spurring west out of town. Garvey must have known that Nevado would come after him and was using the girl as a hostage to ensure his safe passage out of the state.

The gunfighter would have to play it mighty cool when he eventually caught up with them, which he would surely do.

His horse sensed the urgency of the situation and found the extra stamina to maintain a steady and unrelenting pace. Consequently, Nevado had no need of the inducements on his boot heels. With a reluctant hostage in tow, Garvey's own pace would be substantially curtailed.

So it was towards evening when Nevado spotted the two riders in the distance. They were in the lee of Cathedral Butte. Garvey must have been keeping a wary eye on his backtrail for any sign of pursuit.

Suddenly he veered off the well-worn route and headed into the rough lower reaches of the soaring rock promontory, dragging the reluctant prisoner behind.

Even though it was an hour before sundown, lengthening shadows trailed across the arid landscape. Nevado slowed his mount to a walk scanning the desolate terrain for his quarry. The deep-throated boom of a rifle saw him plunging headlong off his horse into the shelter of a cluster of rocks.

The horse trotted off unconcernedly, along with his own long gun. With only the .44 Frontier, he knew that he would have to get in close to take out Wade Garvey. Luckily there was plenty of cover enabling him to circle around behind the fleeing bandit.

Then a gruff voice rang out.

'Come any closer, gunslick, and the girl gets it.'

Nevado judged it to have originated fifty yards over to his left. He was closer than he had expected. Another twenty yards and he would be within pistol range. A cold sweat broke out on his forehead. The brutal threat had made him realize how much he cared for Penny Wilson, and how much he wanted to change in order to accommodate the way of life she had to offer.

Close-mouthed, he held his peace, not wanting to reveal his position. Gingerly and with careful deliberation, he crawled ever closer to the holed-up outlaw. The moment of truth was almost upon him.

But no way could he afford to jeopardize the girl's life.

'If'n you don't come out by the time I count to three,' echoed the menacing threat, 'you can say goodbye to the lovely Miss Wilson . . . One!'

Removing his hat, Nevado peered over the lip of a rock. There was still no sign of the pair.

'Two!'

Nevado could feel himself shaking. Sweating buckets and oozing panic, he knew he couldn't let this happen. There was only one course of action open to him. He prepared to throw out his gun and surrender, knowing full well it meant a bullet in the guts.

'Thr . . . aaaaaaaaagh!'

At that instant, a howl of pain rent the air.

Garvey's head bobbed above the rock behind which he was concealed. Desperately he was attempting to disengage himself from his hostage whose teeth were buried in his neck. The girl clung to him like a limpet but was no match for a brawny hardcase of Garvey's ilk. Throwing her aside, and his attention distracted, he presented the perfect target for the hired gunfighter.

Nevado took full advantage of this heaven-sent opportunity.

The Frontier bucked in his steady hand. Garvey had no chance and went down under the hail of lead. Slowly, the gunfighter rose to his feet and shuffled over to the dying outlaw. His breath was shallow, emerging in short wheezing gulps. He hadn't long for this world and knew it.

'Who . . . are . . . you?' he gasped struggling on to one elbow.

Nevado's smile was cold and pitiless in its intensity. Slowly, purposefully, he took out the gold watch, set it down on a rock and flipped open the lid. The haunting refrain drifted across the arid wilderness.

Garvey's eyes bulged, his slack jaw fell open.

'Now you know,' whispered Nevado. 'Justice has finally been served.'

The shock hammered the final nail in the outlaw's coffin.

After checking that Penny Wilson was unharmed, Nevado slung the dead outlaw across his horse. Then he and the girl retraced their steps back to Buckeye. This time at a far more sedate pace.

It was some time before either spoke.

Nevado eventually broke the tense silence.

'Do you think at some point in the not-too-distant

future there might be a place in your life for an ex
gunfighting man?' he enquired, angling a hesitan
look in the girl's direction.

For some moments she chewed over the question
with exaggerated solicitude before returning hi
anxious frown with one of seemingly equal concern.

'Now there is a question that needs thinking on,
she murmured.